FOUR BY MOORCOCK

'Arioch! Master! I invoke thee, Lord of Chaos!'

Elric shrieked the age-old battle-ululation of
his folk and pressed on to the singing citadel,
slashing at the intangible images that swirled on
all sides. It was the destiny of Elric of the
Black Sword, sorcerer and slayer of kin,
despoiler of the homeland, to be a wanderer
under the power of a destiny greater than he
knew. . . .

*In these four tales, Michael Moorcock
augments the saga of Elric, last ruler of
Melniboné, and relates the strange histories of
Rackhir of Tanelorn, Aubec of Malador and
Simon of Byzantium who sold his sword to the
demented god-king Alexander.*

Also by Michael Moorcock
in Mayflower Books

The Singing Citadel

Four tales of heroic fantasy

Michael Moorcock

Mayflower

Granada Publishing Limited
Published in 1970 by Mayflower Books Ltd
Frogmore, St Albans, Herts AL2 2NF
Reprinted 1973, 1974

These stories first appeared in
Science Fantasy Magazine 1962/3
Fantastic Adventures, June 1964
The Fantastic Swordsman, ed. L Sprague de
Camp, Pyramid Books, USA, 1967
Copyright © Michael Moorcock 1970
Made and printed in Great Britain by
Richard Clay (The Chaucer Press) Ltd
Bungay, Suffolk
Set in Linotype Times

For Doug and Gala Hill

Contents

THE SINGING CITADEL

INTRODUCTION

For ten thousand years did the Bright Empire of Melniboné rule the world by virtue of her sorcerer kings, her dragon hordes, and her golden battle-barges. From Imrryr, the Dreaming City, capital of the Isle of Melniboné, the power of the Bright Emperors radiated over all the lands of mankind, though the Melnibonéans were not true men themselves. They were tall, with eldritch features. They were proud, malicious, sensitive, and artistic, with a vast knowledge of sorcery. They were familiar with many of the supernatural realms of the Higher Worlds and knew that the wonders of Earth could not compare with those of the Higher Worlds. They regarded their late-born cousins of the Young Kingdoms with arrogant contempt, reckoning them fit only to be plundered or enslaved.

But at last, after a hundred centuries, Melniboné's power began to wane as she was shaken by the casting of frightful runes, attacked by powers even greater than she, until all that was left of the Bright Empire was the Isle itself and its single city, Imrryr, still strong, still feared, still the mercantile capital of the world, but no longer the glorious power she had been.

And so it might have remained, save that it was not Destiny's way to have it so.

For the next few centuries, which was called the Age of the Young Kingdoms, petty empires rose and fell and the new nations had their moments of power—Sheegoth, Maidahk, S'aaleem, Ilmiora, and others. And then there came a great movement upon the Earth and above it; the destiny of men and gods was hammered out upon the forge of Fate, and monstrous wars were brewed, and mighty deeds performed. And during this time there rose up many heroes.

Chief of these was Elric, last ruler of Melniboné, who bore the rune-carved black sword, Stormbringer. Hero, perhaps, is not the proper term for Elric, for it was he who turned against his own line and led the Sea Lords of the Young Kingdoms in their mighty attack upon Imrryr—an attack which resulted in Imrryr's destruction and theirs! But it was all part of Fate's plan, though Elric was not to learn this for many years.

Elric of Melniboné, proud prince of ruins, last lord of a dying race, became a wanderer, loathed and feared throughout the lands of the Young Kingdoms. Elric of the Black Sword, sorcerer and slayer of kin, despoiler of his homeland, crimson-eyed albino, who had within him a greater destiny than he knew . . .

The Chronicle of the Black Sword

CHAPTER ONE

The turquoise sea was peaceful in the golden light of early evening, and the two men at the rail of the ship stood in silence, looking north to the misty horizon. One was tall and slim, wrapped in a heavy black cloak, its cowl flung back to reveal his long, milk-white hair; the other was short and red-headed.

'She was a fine woman and she loved you,' said the short man at length. 'Why did you leave her so abruptly?'

'She was a fine woman,' the tall one replied, 'but she would have loved me to her cost. Let her seek her own land and stay there. I have already slain one woman whom I loved, Moonglum. I would not slay another.'

Moonglum shrugged. 'I sometimes wonder, Elric, if this grim destiny of yours is the figment of your own guilt-ridden mood.'

'Perhaps,' Elric replied carelessly. 'But I do not care to test the theory. Let's speak no more of this.'

The sea foamed and rushed by as the oars disrupted the surface, driving the ship swiftly towards the port of Dhakos, capital of Jharkor, one of the most powerful of the Young Kingdoms. Less than two years previously Jharkor's king, Darmit, had died in the ill-fated raid on Imrryr, and Elric had heard that the men of Jharkor blamed him for the young king's death, though this was not the case. He cared little whether they blamed him or not, for he was still disdainful of the greater part of mankind.

'Another hour will see nightfall, and it's unlikely we'll sail at night,' Moonglum said. 'I'll to bed, I think.'

Elric was about to reply when he was interrupted by a high-pitched shout from the crowsnest.

'Sail on larboard stern!'

The lookout must have been half asleep, for the ship bearing down on them could easily be made out from the deck. Elric stepped aside as the captain, a dark-faced Tarkeshite, came running along the deck.

'What's the ship, captain?' called Moonglum.

'A Pan Tang trireme—a warship. They're on ramming course.' The captain ran on, yelling orders to the helm to turn the ship aside.

Elric and Moonglum cross the deck to see the trireme better. She was a black-sailed ship, painted black and heavily gilded, with three rowers to an oar as against their two. She was big and yet elegant, with a high curving stern and a low prow. Now they could see the waters broken by her big, brass-sheathed ram. She had two lateen-rigged sails, and the wind was in her favour.

The rowers were in a panic as they sweated to turn the ship according to the helmsman's orders. Oars rose and fell in confusion and Moonglum turned to Elric with a half-smile

'They'll never do it. Best ready your blade, friend.'

Pan Tang was an isle of sorcerers, fully human, who sought to emulate the old power of Melniboné. Their fleets were among the best in the Young Kingdoms and raided with little discrimination. The Theocrat of Pan Tang, chief of the priest-aristocracy, was Jagreen Lern, who was reputed to have a pact with the powers of Chaos and a plan to rule the world.

Elric regarded the men of Pan Tang as upstarts who could never hope to mirror the glory of his ancestors, but even he had to admit that this ship was impressive and would easily win a fight with the Tarkeshite galley.

Soon the great trireme was bearing down on them and captain and helmsman fell silent as they realised they could not evade the ram. With a harsh sound of crushed timbers, the ram connected with the stern, holing the galley beneath the waterline.

Elric stood immobile, watching as the trireme's grappling

irons hurtled towards their galley's deck. Somewhat half-heartedly, knowing they were no match for the well-trained and well-armoured Pan Tang crew, the Tarkeshites ran towards the stern, preparing to resist the boarders.

Moonglum cried urgently: 'Elric—we must help!'

Reluctantly Elric nodded. He was loathe to draw the rune-sword from its scabbard at his side. The blade was supernatural in origin, semi-sentient. Elric's particular form of albinoism would normally have made him a weakling. But a symbiotic relationship existed between him and the sword—it needed him to wield it and, in return, it sucked the energies of those it slew to feed both itself and Elric. Elric had often speculated on the true nature of the sword, wondered what degree of sentience it possessed, hated it for what it made of him—and, at the same time, needed it if he were to survive.

Now the scarlet-armoured warriors were swinging towards where the Tarkeshites waited. The first wave, armed with broadswords and battle-axes, hit the sailors, driving them back.

Now Elric's hand fell to the hilt of Stormbringer. As he gripped it and drew it, the blade gave an odd, disturbing moan, as if of anticipation, and a weird black radiance seemed to flicker along its length. Now it throbbed in Elric's hand like something alive as the albino ran forward to aid the Tarkeshite sailors.

Already half the defenders had been hewed down and as the rest retreated, Elric, with Moonglum at his heels, moved forward. The scarlet-armoured warriors' expressions changed from grim triumph to startlement as Elric's great black-blade shrieked up and down and clove through a man's armour from shoulder to lower ribs.

Evidently they recognised him and the sword, for both were legendary. Though Moonglum was a skilled swordsman, they all but ignored him as they realised that they must concentrate all their strength on bringing Elric down if they were to survive.

The old, wild killing-lust of his ancestors now dominated Elric as the blade reaped souls. He and the sword became one and it was the sword, not Elric, that was in control. Men fell on all sides, screaming more in horror than in pain as they realised what the sword had drawn from them. Four came at him with axes whistling. He sliced off one's head, cut a deep gash in another's midriff, lopped off an arm, and drove the

10

blade point first into the heart of the last. Now the Tarkeshites were cheering, following after Elric and Moonglum as they cleared the sinking galley's decks of attackers.

Howling like a wolf, Elric grabbed a rope—part of the black and gold trireme's rigging—and swung towards the enemy's decks.

'Follow him!' Moonglum yelled. 'This is our only chance—this ship's doomed!'

The trireme had raised decks fore and aft. On the foredeck stood the captain, splendid in scarlet and blue, his face aghast at this turn of events. He had expected to get his prize effortlessly, now it seemed *he* was to be the prize!

Stormbringer sang a wailing song as Elric pressed towards the foredeck, a song that was at once triumphant and ecstatic. The remaining warriors no longer rushed at him and concentrated on Moonglum, who was leading the Tarkeshite crew, leaving Elric's path to the captain clear.

The captain, a member of the theocracy, would be harder to vanquish than his men. As Elric moved towards him, he noted that the man's armour had a peculair glow to it—it had been sorcerously treated.

The captain was typical of his kind—stocky, heavily-bearded, with malicious black eyes over a strong, hooked nose. His lips were thick and red and he was smiling a little as, with axe in one hand and sword in the other, he prepared to meet Elric, who was running up the steps.

Elric gripped Stormbringer in both hands and lunged for the captain's stomach, but the man stepped sideways and parried with his sword, swinging the axe left-handed at Elric's unprotected head. The albino had to sway to one side, staggered, and fell to the deck, rolling as the broadsword thudded into the deck, just missing his shoulder. Stormbringer seemed to rise of its own accord to block a further axe blow and then chopped upwards to sheer off the head near the handle. The captain cursed and discarded the handle, gripped his broadsword in both hands and raised it. Again Stormbringer acted a fraction sooner than Elric's own reactions. He drove the blade up towards the man's heart. The magic-treated armour stopped it for a second; but then Stormbringer shrilled a chilling, wailing song, shuddered as if summoning more strength, slipped on the armour again. And then the magic armour split like a nutshell, leaving Elric's

11

opponent bare-chested, his arms still raised for the strike. His eyes widened. He backed away, his sword forgotten, his gaze fixed on the evil runeblade as it struck him under the breast-bone and drove in. He grimaced, whimpered, and dropped his sword, clutching instead at the blade, which was sucking out his soul.

'By Chardros—not—not—aahhh!'

He died knowing that even his soul was not safe from the hell-blade borne by the wolf-faced albino.

Elric wrenched Stormbringer from the corpse, feeling his own vitality increase as the sword passed on its stolen energy.

On the deck of the trireme, only the galley-slaves were left alive. But the deck was tilting badly, for the trireme's ram and grapples still tied it to the sinking Tarkeshite ship.

'Cut the grappling ropes and back water—quickly!' Elric yelled. Sailors, realising what was happening, leapt forward to do as he ordered. The slaves backed water, and the ram came out with a groan of split wood. The grapples were cut and the doomed galley set adrift.

Elric counted the survivors. Less than half the crew were alive, and their captain had died in the first onslaught. He addressed the slaves.

'If you'd have your freedom, row well towards Dhakos,' he called. The sun was setting, but now that he was in command he decided to sail through the night by the stars.

Moonglum shouted incredulously: 'Why offer them their freedom? We could sell them in Dhakos and thus be paid for today's exertion!'

Elric shrugged. 'I offer them freedom because I choose to, Moonglum.'

The redhead sighed and turned to supervise the throwing of the dead and wounded overboard. He would never understand the albino, he decided. It was probably for the best.

And that was how Elric came to enter Dhakos in some style, when he had originally intended to slip into the city without being recognised.

Leaving Moonglum to negotiate the sale of the trireme and divide the money between the crew and himself, Elric drew his hood over his head and pushed through the crowd which had collected, making for an inn he knew of by the west gate of the city.

CHAPTER TWO

Later that night, when Moonglum had gone to bed, Elric sat in the tavern room drinking. Even the most enthusiastic of the night's roisterers had left when they had noticed with whom they shared the room; and now Elric sat alone, the only light coming from a guttering reed torch over the outside door.

Now the door opened and a richly-dressed youth stood there, staring in.

'I seek the White Wolf,' he said, his head at a questioning angle. He could not see Elric clearly.

'I'm sometimes called that name in these parts,' Elric said calmly. 'Do you seek Elric of Melniboné?'

'Aye. I have a message.' The youth came in, keeping his cloak wrapped about him, for the room was cold though Elric did not notice it.

'I am Count Yolan, deputy-commander of the city guard,' the youth said arrogantly, coming up to the table at which Elric 'sat and studying the albino rudely. 'You are brave to come here so openly. Do you think the folk of Jharkor have such short memories they can forget that you led their king into a trap scarce two years since?'

Elric sipped his wine, then said from behind the rim of his cup: 'This is rhetoric, Count Yolan. What is your message?'

Yolan's assured manner left him; he made a rather weak gesture. 'Rhetoric to you, perhaps—but I for one feel strongly on the matter. Would not King Darmit be here today if you had not fled from the battle that broke the power of the Sea Lord and your own folk? Did you not use your sorcery to aid you in your flight, instead of using it to aid the men who thought they were your comrades?'

Elric sighed. 'I know your purpose here was not to bait me in this manner. Darmit died on board his flagship during the first attack on Imrryr's sea-maze, not in the subsequent battle.'

'You sneer at my questions and then proffer lame lies to cover your own cowardly deed,' Yolan said bitterly. 'If I had my way you'd be fed to your hell-blade there—I've heard what happened earlier.'

Elric rose slowly. 'Your taunts tire me. When you feel ready

13

to deliver your message, give it to the inn-keeper.'

He walked around the table, moving towards the stairs, but stopped as Yolan turned and plucked at his sleeve.

Elric's corpse-white face stared down at the young noble. His crimson eyes flickered with a dangerous emotion. 'I am not used to such familiarity, young man.'

Yolan's hand fell away. 'Forgive me. I was self-indulgent and should not have let my emotions override diplomacy. I came on a matter of discretion—a message from Queen Yishana. She seeks your help.'

'I'm as disinclined to help others as I am to explain my actions,' Elric spoke impatiently. 'In the past my help has not always been to the advantage of those who've sought it. Darmit, your queen's half-brother, discovered that.'

Yolan said sullenly: 'You echo my own warnings to the queen, sir. For all that, she desires to see you in private—tonight...' he scowled and looked away. 'I would point out that I could have you arrested should you refuse.'

'Perhaps.' Elric moved again towards the steps. 'Tell Yishana that I stay the night here and move on at dawn. She may visit me if her request is so urgent.' He climbed the stairs, leaving a gape-mouthed Yolan sitting alone in the quiet of the tavern.

Theleb K'aarna scowled. For all his skill in the black arts, he was a fool in love; and Yishana, sprawled on her fur-rich bed, knew it. It pleased her to have power over a man who could destroy her with a simple incantation if it were not for his love-weakness. Though Theleb K'aarna stood high in the hierarchy of Pan Tang, it was clear to her that she was in no danger from the sorcerer. Indeed, her intuition informed her that this man who loved to dominate others also needed to be dominated. She filled this need for him—with relish.

Theleb K'aarna continued to scowl at her. 'How can that decadent spell-singer help you where I cannot?' he muttered, sitting down on the bed and stroking her bejewelled foot.

Yishana was not a young woman, neither was she pretty. Yet there was an hypnotic quality about her tall, full body, her lush black hair, and her wholly sensuous face. Few of the men she had singled out for her pleasure had been able to resist her.

Neither was she sweet-natured, just, wise, nor self-sacrific-
ing. The historians would append no noble soubriquet to her
name. Still, there was something so self-sufficient about her,
something denying the usual standards by which a person was
judged, that all who knew her admired her, and she was well-
loved by those she ruled—loved rather as a wilful child is
loved, yet loved with firm loyalty.

Now she laughed quietly, mockingly at her sorcerer lover.

'You're probably right, Theleb K'aarna, but Elric is a legend
—the most spoken-of, least-known man in the world. This is
my opportunity to discover what others have only speculated
on—his true character.'

Theleb K'aarna made a pettish gesture. He stroked his long
black beard and got up, walking to a table bearing fruit and
wine. He poured wine for them both. 'If you seek to make me
jealous again, you are succeeding, of course. I hold little hope
for your ambition. Elric's ancestors were half-demons—his
race is not human and cannot be judged by our yardsticks. To
us, sorcery is learned after years of study and sacrifice—to
Elric's kind, sorcery is intuitive—natural. You may not live to
learn his secrets. Cymoril, his beloved cousin, died on his blade
—and she was his betrothed!'

'Your concern is touching.' She lazily accepted the goblet he
handed to her. 'But I'll continue with my plan, none the less.
After all, you can hardly claim to have had much success in
discovering the nature of this citadel!'

'There are subtleties I have not properly plumbed as yet!'

'Then perhaps Elric's intuition will provide answers where
you fail,' she smiled. Then he got up and looked through the
window at the sky where the full moon hung in a clear sky
over the spires of Dhakos. 'Yolan is late. If all went properly,
he should have brought Elric here by now.'

'Yolan was a mistake. You should not have sent such a close
friend of Darmit's. For all we know, he's challenged Elric and
killed him!'

Again she couldn't resist laughter. 'Oh, you wish too hard—
it clouds your reason. I sent Yolan because I knew he would be
rude to the albino and perhaps weaken his usual insouciance—
arouse his curiosity. Yolan was a kind of bait to bring Elric to
us!'

'Then possibly Elric sensed this?'

'I am not overly intelligent, my love—but I think my instincts rarely betray me. We shall see soon.'

A little later there was a discreet scratch at the door and a handmaiden entered.

'Your Highness, Count Yolan has returned.'

'Only Count Yolan?' There was a smile on Theleb K'aarna's face. It was to disappear in a short while as Yishana left the room, garbed for the street.

'You are a fool!' he snarled as the door slammed. He flung down his goblet. Already he had been unsuccessful in the matter of the citadel and, if Elric displaced him, he could lose everything. He began to think very deeply, very carefully.

CHAPTER THREE

Though he claimed lack of conscience, Elric's tormented eyes belied the claim as he sat at his window, drinking strong wine and thinking on the past. Since the sack of Imrryr, he had quested the world, seeking some purpose to his existence, some meaning to his life.

Recently he had sought the answer in the Dead God's Book, a legendary tome said to hold all the secrets of the universe, only to find the book turned to dust. He had tried to love Shaarilla, the wingless woman of Myyrrhn, trying to forget Cymoril, who still inhabited his nightmares. But he had failed and had left her.

Peace, he thought, was all he sought. Yet even peace in death was denied him. It was in this mood that he continued to brood until his reverie was broken by a soft scratching at the door.

Immediately his expression hardened. His crimson eyes took on a guarded look, his shoulders lifted so that when he stood up he was all cool arrogance. He placed the cup on the table and said lightly:

'Enter!'

A woman entered, swathed in a dark red cloak, unrecognisable in the gloom of the room. She closed the door behind her and stood there, motionless and unspeaking.

16

When at length she spoke, her voice was almost hesitant, though there was some irony in it, too.

'You sit in darkness, Lord Elric, I had thought to find you asleep . . .'

'Sleep, madam, is the occupation that bores me most. But I will light a torch if you find the darkness unattractive.' He went to the table and removed the cover from the small bowl of charcoal which lay there. He reached for a thin wooden spill and placed one end in the bowl, blowing gently. Soon the charcoal glowed, and the taper caught, and he touched it to a reed torch that hung in a bracket on the wall above the table.

The torch flared and sent shadows skipping around the small chamber. The woman drew back her cowl and the light caught her dark, heavy features and the masses of black hair which framed them. She contrasted strongly with the slender, aesthetic albino who stood a head taller, looking at her impassively.

She was unused to impassive looks and the novelty pleased her.

'You sent for me, Lord Elric—and you see I am here.' She made a mock curtsey.

'Queen Yishana,' he acknowledged the curtsey with a slight bow. Now that she confronted him, she sensed his power—a power that perhaps attracted even more strongly than her own. And yet, he gave no hint that he responded to her. She reflected that a situation she had expected to be interesting might, ironically, become frustrating. Even this amused her.

Elric, in turn, was intrigued by this woman in spite of himself. His jaded emotions hinted that Yishana might restore their edge. This excited him and perturbed him at once.

He relaxed a little and shrugged. 'I have heard of you, Queen Yishana, in other lands than Jharkor. Sit down if you wish.' He indicated a bench and seated himself on the edge of the bed.

'You are more courteous than your summons suggested,' she smiled as she sat down, crossed her legs, and folded her arms in front of her. 'Does this mean that you will listen to a proposition I have?'

He smiled back. It was a rare smile for him, a little grim, but without the usual bitterness. 'I think so. You are an unusual woman, Queen Yishana. Indeed, I would suspect that you had

17

Melnibonéan blood if I did not know better.'

'Not all your Young Kingdom "upstarts" are quite as unsophisticated as you believe, my lord.'

'Perhaps.'

'Now that I see you at last, face to face, I find your dark legend a little hard to credit in parts—and yet, on the other hand,' she put her head on one side and regarded him frankly, 'it would seem that the legends speak of a less subtle man than the one I see before me.'

'That is the way with legends.'

'Ah,' she half-whispered, 'what a force we could be together, you and I . . .'

'Speculation of that sort irritates me, Queen Yishana. What is your purpose in coming here?'

'Very well. I did not expect you to listen, even.'

'I'll listen—but expect nothing more.'

'Then listen. I think the story will be appreciated, even by you.'

Elric listened and, as Yishana had suspected, the tale she told began to catch his interest . . .

Several months ago, Yishana told Elric, peasants in the Gharavian province of Jharkor began to talk of some mysterious riders who were carrying off young men and women from the villages.

Suspecting bandits, Yishana had sent a detachment of her White Leopards, Jharkor's finest fighting men, to the province to put down the brigands.

None of the White Leopards had returned. A second expedition had found no trace of them but, in a valley close to the town of Thokora, they had come upon a strange citadel. Descriptions of the citadel were confused. Suspecting that the White Leopards had attacked and been defeated, the officer in charge had used discretion, left a few men to watch the citadel and report anything they saw, and returned at once to Dhakos. One thing was certain—the citadel had not been in the valley a few months before.

Yishana and Theleb K'aarna had led a large force to the valley. The men left behind had disappeared but, as soon as he saw the citadel, Theleb K'aarna had warned Yishana not to attack.

'It was a marvellous sight, Lord Elric,' Yishana continued. 'The citadel scintillated with shining, rainbow colours—colours that were constantly altering, shifting, changing. The whole building looked unreal—sometimes it stood out sharply; sometimes it seemed misty, as if about to vanish. Theleb K'aarna said its nature was sorcerous, and we did not doubt him. Something from the Realm of Chaos, he said, and that seemed likely.' She got up.

She spread her hands. 'We are not used to large-scale manifestations of sorcery in these parts. Theleb K'aarna was familiar enough with sorcery—he comes from the City of Screaming Statues on Pan Tang, and such things are seen frequently—but even he was taken aback.'

'So you withdrew,' Elric prompted impatiently.

'We were about to—in fact Theleb K'aarna and myself were already riding back at the head of the army when the music came ... It was sweet, beautiful, unearthly, painful—Theleb K'aarna shouted to me to ride as swiftly as I could away from it. I dallied, attracted by the music, but he slapped the rump of my horse and we rode, fast as dragons in flight, away from there. Those nearest us also escaped—but we saw the rest turn and move back towards the citadel, drawn by the music. Nearly two hundred men went back—and vanished.'

'What did you do then?' Elric asked as Yishana crossed the floor and sat down beside him. He moved to give her more room.

'Theleb K'aarna has been trying to investigate the nature of the citadel—its purpose and its controller. So far, his divinations have told him little more than he guessed: that the Realm of Chaos has sent the citadel to the Realm of Earth and is slowly extending its range. More and more of our young men and women are being abducted by the minions of Chaos.'

'And these minions?' Yishana had moved a little closer, and this time Elric did not move away.

'None who has sought to stop them has succeeded—few have lived.'

'And what do you seek of me?'

'Help.' She looked closely into his face and reached out a hand to touch him. 'You have knowledge of both Chaos and Law—old knowledge, instinctive knowledge if Theleb K'aarna is right. Why, your very Gods are Lords of Chaos.'

19

'That is exactly true, Yishana—and because our patron Gods are of Chaos, it is not in my interest to fight against any one of them.'

Now he moved towards her and he was smiling, looking into her eyes. Suddenly, he took her in his arms. 'Perhaps you will be strong enough,' he said enigmatically, just before their lips met. 'And as for the other matter—we can discuss that later.'

In the deep greenness of a dark mirror, Theleb K'aarna saw something of the scene in Elric's room and he glowered impotently. He tugged at his beard as the scene faded for the tenth time in a minute. This time none of his mutterings could restore it. He sat back in his chair of serpent skulls and planned vengeance. That vengeance could take time maturing, he decided; for, if Elric could be useful in the matter of the citadel, there was no point in destroying him yet. . . .

CHAPTER FOUR

Next afternoon, three riders set off for the town of Thokora. Elric and Yishana rode close together; but the third rider, Theleb K'aarna, kept a frowning distance. If Elric was at all embarrassed by this display on the part of the man he had ousted in Yishana's affections, he did not show it.

Elric, finding Yishana more than attractive, in spite of himself, had agreed at least to inspect the citadel and suggest what it might be and how it might be fought. He had exchanged a few words with Moonglum before setting off.

They rode across the beautiful grasslands of Jharkor, golden beneath a hot sun. It was two days' ride to Thokora, and Elric intended to enjoy it.

Feeling less than miserable, he galloped along with Yishana, laughing with her in her enjoyment. Yet, buried deeper than it would normally have been, there was a deep foreboding in his heart as they neared the mysterious citadel, and he noted that Theleb K'aarna occasionally looked satisfied when he should have looked disgruntled.

Sometimes Elric would shout to the sorcerer. 'Ho, old spellmaker, do you feel no joyful release from the cares of the court out here amidst the beauties of nature? Your face is long, Theleb K'aarna—breathe in the untainted air and laugh with us!' Then Theleb K'aarna would scowl and mutter, and Yishana would laugh at him and glance brightly at Elric.

So they came to Thokora and found it a smouldering pit that stank like a midden of hell.

Elric sniffed. 'This is Chaos work. You were right enough there, Theleb K'aarna. Whatever fire destroyed such a large town, it was not natural fire. Whoever is responsible for this is evidently increasing its power. As you know, sorcerer, the Lords of Law and Chaos are usually in perfect balance, neither tampering directly with our Earth. Evidently the balance has tipped a little way to one side, as it sometimes does, favouring the Lords of Disorder—allowing them access to our realm. Normally it is possible for an earthly sorcerer to summon aid from Chaos or Law for a short time, but it is rare for either side to establish itself so firmly as our friend in the citadel evidently has. What is more disturbing—for you of the Young Kingdoms, at least—is that, once such power is gained, it is possible to increase it, and the Lords of Chaos could in time conquer the Realm of Earth by gradual increase of their strength here.'

'A terrible possibility,' muttered the sorcerer, genuinely afraid. Even though he could sometimes summon help from Chaos, it was in no human being's interest to have Chaos ruling over him.

Elric climbed back into his saddle. 'We'd best make speed to the valley,' he said.

'Are you sure it is wise, after witnessing this?' Theleb K'aarna was nervous.

Elric laughed. 'What? And you a sorcerer from Pan Tang— that isle that claims to know as much of sorcery as my ancestors, the Bright Emperors! No, no—besides, I'm not in a cautious mood today!'

'Nor am I,' cried Yishana, clapping her steed's sides. 'Come, gentlemen—to the Citadel of Chaos!'

By late afternoon, they had topped the range of hills surrounding the valley and looked down at the mysterious citadel.

Yishana had described it well—but not perfectly. Elric's eyes ached as he looked at it, for it seemed to extend beyond the Realm of Earth into a different plane, perhaps several.

It shimmered and glittered and all Earthly colours were there, as well as many which Elric recognised as belonging to other planes. Even the basic outline of the citadel was uncertain. In contrast, the surrounding valley was a sea of dark ash, which sometimes seemed to eddy, to undulate and send up spurting geysers of dust, as if the basic elements of nature had been disturbed, and warped by the presence of the supernatural citadel.

'Well?' Theleb K'aarna tried to calm his nervous horse as it backed away from the citadel. 'Have you seen the like in the world before?'

Elric shook his head. 'Not in this world, certainly; but I've seen it before. During my final initiation into the arts of Melniboné, my father took me with him in astral form to the Realm of Chaos, there to receive the audience of my patron the Lord Arioch of the Seven Darks...'

Theleb K'aarna shuddered. 'You have been to Chaos? It is Arioch's citadel, then?'

Elric laughed in disdain. 'That! No, it is a hovel compared to the palaces of the Lords of Chaos.'

Impatiently, Yishana said: 'Then who dwells *there*?'

'As I remember, the one who dwelt in the citadel when I passed through the Chaos Realm in my youth—he was no Lord of Chaos, but a kind of servant to the Lords. Yet,' he frowned, 'not exactly a servant....'

'*Ach!* You speak in riddles.' Theleb K'aarna turned his horse to ride down the hills, away from the citadel. 'I know you Melnibonéans! Starving, you'd rather have a paradox than food!'

Elric and Yishana followed him some distance, then Elric stopped. Elric pointed behind him.

'The one who dwells yonder is a paradoxical sort of fellow. He's a kind of Jester to the Court of Chaos. The Lords of Chaos respect him—perhaps fear him slightly—even though he entertains them. He delights them with cosmic riddles, with farcical satires purporting to explain the nature of the Cosmic Hand that holds both Chaos and Law in balance, he juggles enigmas like baubles, laughs at what Chaos holds dear, takes seriously that which they mock at...' He paused and shrugged. 'So I have heard, at least.'

'Why should he be here?'

'Why should he be anywhere? I could guess at the motives of Chaos or Law and probably be right. But not even the Lords of the Higher Worlds can understand the motives of Balo the Jester. It is said that he is the only one allowed to move between the Realms of Chaos and Law at will, though I have never heard of him coming to the Realm of Earth before. Neither, for that matter, have I ever heard him credited with such acts of destruction as that which we've witnessed. It is a puzzle to me—one which would no doubt please him if he knew.'

'There would be one way of discovering the purpose of his visit,' Theleb K'aarna said with a faint smile. 'If someone entered the citadel . . .'

'Come now, sorcerer,' Elric mocked. 'I've little love for life, to be sure, but there are some things of value to me—my soul, for one!'

Theleb K'aarna began to ride on down the hill, but Elric remained thoughtfully where he was, Yishana beside him.

'You seem more troubled by this than you should be, Elric,' she said.

'It *is* disturbing. There is a hint here that, if we investigate the citadel further, we should become embroiled in some dispute between Balo and his masters—perhaps even the Lords of Law, too. To become so involved could easily mean our destruction, since the forces at work are more dangerous and powerful than anything we are familiar with on Earth.'

'But we cannot simply watch this Balo laying our cities waste, carrying off our fairest, threatening to rule Jharkor himself within a short time!'

Elric sighed, but did not reply.

'Have you no sorcery, Elric, to send Balo back to Chaos where he belongs, to seal the breach he has made in our Realm?'

'Even Melnibonéans cannot match the power of the Lords of the Higher Worlds—and my forefathers knew much more of sorcery than do I. My best allies serve neither Chaos nor Law, they are elementals: lords of fire, earth, air, and water, entities with affinities with beasts and plants. Good allies in an earthly battle—but of no great use when matched against one such as Balo. I must think.... At least, if I opposed Balo it would not necessarily incur the wrath of my patron Lords. Something, I suppose....'

The hills rolled green and lush to the grasslands at their feet, the sun beat down from a clear sky on the infinity of grass stretching to the horizon. Above them a large predatory bird wheeled; and Theleb K'aarna was a tiny figure, turning in the saddle to call to them in a thin voice, but his words could not be heard.

Yishana seemed dispirited. Her shoulders slightly slumped, and she did not look at Elric as she began to guide her horse slowly down towards the sorcerer of Pan Tang. Elric followed, conscious of his own indecision, yet half-careless of it. What did it matter to him if ... ?

The music began, faintly at first, but beginning to swell with an attractive, poignant sweetness, evoking nostalgic memories, offering peace and giving life a sharp meaning, all at once. If the music came from instruments, then they were not earthly. It produced in him a yearning to turn about and discover its source, but he resisted it. Yishana, on the other hand, was evidently not finding the music so easily resisted. She had wheeled completely round, her face radiant, her lips trembling and tears shining in her eyes.

Elric, in his wanderings in unearthly realms, had heard music like it before—it echoed many of the bizarre symphonies of old Melniboné—and it did not draw him as it drew Yishana. He recognised swiftly that she was in danger, and as she came past him, spurring her horse, he reached out to grab her bridle.

Her whip slashed at his hand and, cursing with unexpected pain, he dropped the bridle. She went past him, galloping up to the crest of the hill and vanishing over it in an instant.

'Yishana!' He shouted at her desperately, but his voice would not carry over the pulsing music. He looked back, hoping that Theleb K'aarna would lend help, but the sorcerer was riding rapidly away. Evidently, on hearing the music, he had come to a swift decision.

Elric raced after Yishana, screaming for her to turn back. His own horse reached the top of the hill and he saw her bent over her steed's neck as she goaded it towards the shining citadel.

'Yishana! You go to your doom!'

24

Now she had reached the outer limits of the citadel, and her horse's feet seemed to strike off shimmering waves of colour as they touched the Chaos-disturbed ground surrounding the place. Although he knew it was too late to stop her, Elric continued to speed after her, hoping to reach her before she entered the citadel itself.

But, even as he entered the rainbow swirl, he saw what appeared to be a dozen Yishanas going through a dozen gateways into the citadel. Oddly refracted light created the illusion and made it impossible to tell which was the real Yishana.

With Yishana's disappearance the music stopped and Elric thought he heard a faint whisper of laughter following it. His horse was by this time becoming increasingly difficult to control, and he did not trust himself to it. He dismounted, his legs wreathed in radiant mist, and let the horse go. It galloped off, snorting its terror.

Elric's left hand moved to the hilt of his runesword, but he hesitated to draw it. Once pulled from its scabbard, the blade would demand souls before it allowed itself to be resheathed. Yet it was his only weapon. He withdrew his hand, and the blade seemed to quiver angrily at his side.

'Not yet, Stormbringer. There may be forces within who are stronger even than you!'

He began to wade through the faintly-resisting light swirls. He was half-blinded by the scintillating colours around him, which sometimes shone dark blue, silver, and red; sometimes gold, light green, amber. He also felt the sickening lack of any sort of orientation—distance, depth, breadth were meaningless. He recognised what he had only experienced in an astral form—the odd, timeless, spaceless quality that marked a Realm of the Higher Worlds.

He drifted, pushing his body in the direction in which he guessed Yishana had gone, for by now he had lost sight of the gateway or any of its mirage images.

He realised that, unless he was doomed to drift here until he starved, he must draw Stormbringer; for the runeblade, forged itself by Chaos, could resist the influence of Chaos.

This time, when he gripped the sword's hilt, he felt a shock run up his arm and infuse his body with vitality. The sword came free from the scabbard. From the huge blade, carved with strange old runes, a black radiance poured, meeting the shifting colours of Chaos and dispersing them.

Now Elric shrieked the age-old battle-ululation of his folk and pressed on into the citadel, slashing at the intangible images that swirled on all sides. The gateway was ahead, and Elric knew it now, for his sword had shown him which were the mirages. It was open as Elric reached the portal. He paused for a moment, his lips moving as he remembered an invocation that he might need later. Arioch, Lord of Chaos, patron god-demon of his ancestors, was a negligent power and whimful—he could not rely on Arioch to aid him here, unless . . .

In slow graceful strides, a golden beast with eyes of ruby-fire was loping down the passage that led from the portal. Bright though the eyes were, they seemed blind, and its huge, doglike muzzle was closed. Yet its path could only lead it to Elric and, as it neared him, the mouth suddenly gaped showing coral fangs. In silence it came to a halt, the blind eyes never once settling on the albino, and then sprang!

Elric staggered back, raising the sword in defence. He was flung to the ground by the beast's weight and felt its body cover him. It was cold, cold, and it made no attempt to savage him—just lay on top of him and let the cold permeate his body.

Elric began to shiver as he pushed at the chilling body of the beast. Stormbringer moaned and murmured in his hand, and then it pierced some part of the beast's body, and a horrible cold strength began to fill the albino. Reinforced by the beast's own life-force, he heaved upwards. The beast continued to smother him, though now a thin, barely audible sound was coming from it. Elric guessed that Stormbringer's small wound was hurting the creature.

Desperately, for he was shaking and aching with cold, he moved the sword and stabbed again. Again the thin sound from the beast; again cold energy flooded through him, and again he heaved. This time the beast was flung off and crawled back towards the portal. Elric sprang up, raised Stormbringer high, and brought the sword down on the golden creature's skull. The skull shattered as ice might shatter.

Elric ran forward into the passage and, once within, the place became filled with roars and shrieks that echoed and were magnified. It was as if the voice that the cold beast had lacked outside was shouting its death-agonies here.

Now the floor rose until he was running up a spiral ramp. Looking down, he shuddered, for he looked into an infinite pit of subtle, dangerous colours that swam about in such a way that he could hardly take his eyes from them. He even felt his body begin to leave the ramp and go towards the pit, but he strengthened his grip on the sword and disciplined himself to climb on.

Upwards, as he looked, was the same as downwards. Only the ramp had any kind of constancy, and this began to take on the appearance of a thinly-cut jewel, through which he could see the pit and in which it was reflected.

Greens and blues and yellows predominated, but there were also traces of dark red, black, and orange, and many other colours not in an ordinary human spectrum.

Elric knew he was in some province of the Higher Worlds and guessed that it would not be long before the ramp led him to new danger.

Danger did not seem to await him when at last he came to the end of the ramp and stepped on to a bridge of similar stuff, which led over the scintillating pit to an archway that shone with a steady blue light.

He crossed the bridge cautiously and as cautiously entered the arch. Everything was blue-tinged here, even himself; and he trod on, the blue becoming deeper and deeper as he progressed.

Then Stormbringer began to murmur and, either warned by the sword or by some sixth sense of his own, Elric wheeled to his right. Another archway had appeared there and from this there began to shine a light as deep red as the other was blue. Where the two met was a purple of fantastic richness and Elric stared at this, experiencing a similar hypnotic pull as he had had when climbing the ramp. Again his mind was stronger, and he forced himself to enter the red arch. At once another arch appeared to his left, sending a beam of green light to merge with the red, and another to his left brought yellow light, one ahead brought mauve until he seemed trapped within the criss-cross of beams. He slashed at them with Stormbringer, and the black radiance reduced the beams for a moment to streamers of light, which reformed again. Elric continued to move forward.

Now, looming through the confusion of colour, a shape

appeared and Elric thought it was that of a man.

Man it was in shape—but not in size it seemed. Yet, when it drew closer, it was no giant—less than Elric's height. Still it gave the *impression* of vast proportions, rather as if it *were* a giant and Elric had grown to its size.

It blundered towards Elric and went *through* him. It was not that the man was intangible—it was Elric who felt the ghost. The creature's mass seemed of incredible density. The creature was turning, its huge hands reaching out, its face a mocking grimace. Elric struck at it with Stormbringer and was astonished as the runesword was halted, making no impression on the creature's bulk.

Yet when it grasped Elric, its hands went through him. Elric backed away, grinning now in relief. Then he saw with some terror that the light was gleaming through him. He had been right—*he* was the ghost!

The creature reached out for him again, grabbed him again, failed to hold him.

Elric, conscious that he was in no physical danger from the monster, yet also highly conscious that his sanity was about to be permanently impaired, turned and fled.

Quite suddenly he was in a hall, the walls of which were of the same unstable, shifting colours as the rest of the place. But sitting on a stool in the centre of the hall, holding in his hands some tiny creatures that seemed to be running about on his palm, was a small figure who looked up at Elric and grinned merrily.

'Welcome, King of Melniboné. And how fares the last ruler of my favourite earthly race?'

The figure was dressed in shimmering motley. On his head was a tall, spiked crown—a travesty of and a comment upon the crowns of the mighty. His face was angular and his mouth wide.

'Greetings, Lord Balo,' Elric made a mock bow. 'Strange hospitality you offer in your welcome.'

'Ahaha—it did not amuse you, eh? Men are so much harder to please than the gods—you would not think it, would you?'

'Men's pleasures are rarely so elaborate. Where is Queen Yishana?'

'Allow me my pleasures also, mortal. Here she is, I think.' Balo plucked at one of the tiny creatures on his palm. Elric stepped forward and saw that Yishana was indeed there, as were many of the lost soldiers. Balo looked up at him and winked. 'There are so much easier to handle in this size.'

'I do not doubt it, though I wonder if it is not we who are larger rather than they who are smaller....'

'You are astute, mortal. But can you guess how this came to be?'

'Your creature back there—your pits and colours and archways—somehow they warp—what?'

'*Mass*, King Elric. But you would not understand such concepts. Even the Lords of Melniboné, most godlike and intelligent of mortals, only learned how to manipulate the elements in ritual, invocation, and spell, but never understood what they manipulated—that is where the Lords of the Higher Worlds score, whatever their differences.'

'But I survived without need for spells. I survived by disciplining my mind!'

'That helped, for certain—but you forget your greatest asset —that disturbing blade there. You use it in your petty problems to aid you, and you never realise that it is like making use of a mighty war galley to catch a sprat. That sword represents power in *any* Realm, King Elric!'

'Aye, so it might. This does not interest me. Why are you here, Lord Balo?'

Balo chuckled, his laughter rich and musical. 'Oho, I am in disgrace. I quarrelled with my masters, who took exception to a joke of mine about their insignificance and egotism, about their destiny and their pride. Bad taste to them, King, is any hint of their own oblivion. I made a joke in bad taste. I fled from the Higher Worlds to Earth, where, unless invoked, the Lords of Law or Chaos can rarely interfere. You will like my intention, Elric, as would any Melnibonéan—I intend to establish my own Realm on Earth—the Realm of Paradox. A little from Law, a little from Chaos—a Realm of opposites, of curiosities and jokes.'

'I'm thinking we already have such a world as you describe, Lord Balo, with no need for you to create it!'

'Earnest irony, King Elric, for an insouciant man of Melniboné.'

'Ah, that it may be. I am a boor on occasions such as these. Will you release Yishana and myself?'

'But you and I are giants—I have given you the status and appearance of a god. You and I could be partners in this enterprise of mine!'

'Unfortunately, Lord Balo, I do not possess your range of humour and am unfitted for such an exalted role. Besides,' Elric grinned suddenly, 'it is in my mind that the Lords of the Higher Worlds will not easily let drop the matter of your ambition, since it appears to conflict so strongly with theirs.'

Balo laughed but said nothing.

Elric also smiled, but it was an attempt to hide his racing thoughts. 'What do you intend to do if I refuse?'

'Why, Elric, you would not refuse! I can think of many subtle pranks that I could play on you . . .'

'Indeed? And the Black Swords?'

'Ah, yes . . .'

'Balo, in your mirth and obsessions you have not considered everything thoroughly. You should have exerted more effort to vanquish me before I came here.'

Now Elric's eyes gleamed hot and he lifted the sword, crying:

'Arioch! Master! I invoke thee, Lord of Chaos!'

Balo started. 'Cease that, King Elric!'

'Arioch—here is a soul for you to claim!'

'Quiet, I say!'

'Arioch! Hear me!' Elric's voice was loud and desperate.

Balo let his tiny playthings fall and rose hurriedly, skipping towards Elric.

'Your invocation is unheeded!' He laughed, reaching out for Elric. But Stormbringer moaned and shuddered in Elric's hand and Balo withdrew his hand. His face became serious and frowning.

'Arioch of the Seven Darks—your servant calls you!'

The walls of flame trembled and began to fade. Balo's eyes widened and jerked this way and that.

'Oh, Lord Arioch—come reclaim your straying Balo!'

'You cannot!' Balo scampered across the room where one section of the flame had faded entirely, revealing darkness beyond.

'Sadly for you, little jester, he can . . .' The voice was sardonic and yet beautiful. From the darkness stepped a tall figure. As was the custom of the Lords of the Higher Worlds when they visited Earth, the figure was in human guise. Yet the great beauty of the newcomer, filled as it was with a kind of compassion mingled with pride, cruelty, and sadness, showed at once that he could not be human. He was clad in doublet of pulsing scarlet, hose of ever-changing hue, a long golden sword at his hips. His eyes were large, but slanted high, his hair was long and as golden as the sword, his lips were full and his chin pointed like his ears.

'Arioch!' Balo stumbled backwards as the Lord of Chaos advanced.

'It was your mistake, Balo,' Elric said from behind the jester. 'Did you not realise only the Kings of Melniboné may invoke Arioch and bring him to the Realm of Earth? It has been their age-old privilege.'

'And much have they abused it,' said Arioch, smiling faintly as Balo grovelled. 'However, this service you have done us, Elric, will make up for past misuses.'

Even Elric felt awed by the incredibly powerful presence of the Chaos Lord. He also felt much relieved, for he had not been sure that Arioch could be summoned in person. More than once he had called for Arioch's aid and sometimes it had been sent—but this was the first time the Lord of the Higher Worlds had deigned to come himself.

Now Arioch stretched an arm down towards Balo and lifted the jester by his collar so that he jerked and struggled in the air, his face writhing in fear and consternation.

Arioch took hold of Balo's head and squeezed it. Elric looked on in amazement as the head began to shrink. Arioch took Balo's legs and bent them in, folding Balo up and kneading him in his slender, inhuman hands until he was a small, solid ball. Arioch then popped the ball into his mouth and swallowed it.

'I have not eaten him, Elric,' he said with another faint smile. 'It is merely the easiest way of transporting him back to the Realms from which he came. He has transgressed and will be punished. All this'—he waved an arm to indicate the citadel —'is unfortunate and contradicts the plans we of Chaos have for Earth—plans which will involve you, our servant, and make you mighty.'

Elric bowed to his master. 'I am honoured, Lord Arioch, though I seek no favours.'

31

Arioch's silvery voice lost some of its beauty and his face seemed to cloud for a second. 'You are pledged to serve Chaos, Elric, as were your ancestors. You *will* serve Chaos! The time draws near when both Law and Chaos will battle for the Realm of Earth—and Chaos shall win! Earth will be incorporated into our Realm and you will join the hierarchy of Chaos, become immortal as we are!'

'Immortality offers little to me, my lord.'

'Ah, Elric, have the men of Melniboné become as the half-apes who now dominate Earth with their puny "civilisations"? Are you no better then these Young Kingdom upstarts? Think what we offer!'

'I shall, my lord, when the time you mention comes.' Elric's head was still lowered.

'You shall indeed.' Arioch raised his arms. 'Now to transport this toy of Balo's to its proper Realm, and redress the trouble he has caused, lest some hint reaches our opponents before the proper time.'

Arioch's voice swelled like the singing of a million brazen bells and Elric sheathed his sword and clapped his hands over his ears to stop the pain.

Then Elric felt his body seem to *shred* apart, swell and stretch until it became like smoke drifting on air. Then, faster, the smoke began to be drawn together, becoming denser and denser and he seemed to be shrinking now. All around him were rolling banks of colour, flashes and indescribable noises. Then came a vast blackness and he closed his eyes against the images that seemed reflected in the blackness.

When he opened them he stood in the valley and the singing citadel was gone. Only Yishana and a few surprised-looking soldiers stood there. Yishana ran towards him.

'Elric—was it you who saved us?'

'I must claim only part of the credit,' he said.

'Not all my soldiers are here,' she said, inspecting the men. 'Where are the rest—and the villagers abducted earlier?'

'If Balo's tastes are like his masters', then I fear they now have the honour of being part of a demigod. The Lords of Chaos are not flesh-eaters, of course, being of the Higher Worlds, but there is something they savour in men which satisfies them ...'

Yishana hugged her body as if in cold. 'He was huge—I

cannot believe that his citadel could contain his bulk!'

'The citadel was more than a dwelling-place, that was obvious. Somehow it changed size, shape—and other things I cannot describe. Arioch of Chaos transported it and Balo back to where they belong.'

'Arioch! But he is one of the Greatest Six! How did he come to Earth?'

'An old pact with my remote ancestors. By calling him they allow him to spend a short time in our realm, and he repays them with some favour. This was done.'

'Come, Elric,' she took his arm. 'Let's away from the valley.'

Elric was weak and enfeebled by the efforts of summoning Arioch, and the experiences he had had before and since the episode. He could hardly walk; and soon it was Yishana who supported him as they made slow progress, the dazed warriors following in their wake, towards the nearest village, where they could obtain rest and horses to take them back to Dhakos.

CHAPTER FIVE

As they staggered past the blasted ruins of Thokara, Yishana pointed suddenly at the sky.

'What is that?'

A great shape was winging its way towards them. It had the appearance of a butterfly, but a butterfly with wings so huge they blotted out the sun.

'Can it be some creature of Balo's left behind?' she speculated.

'Hardly likely,' he replied. 'This has the appearance of a monster conjured by a human sorcerer.'

'Theleb K'aarna!'

'He has surpassed himself,' Elric said wryly. 'I did not think him capable.'

'It is his vengeance on us, Elric!'

'That seems reasonable. But I am weak, Yishana—and Stormbringer needs souls if it is to replenish my strength.' He turned a calculating eye on the warriors behind him who were gaping up at the creature as it came nearer. Now they could see it had a man's body, covered with hairs or feathers hued like a peacock's.

The air whistled as it descended, its fifty-foot wings dwarfing the seven feet of head and body. From its head grew two curling horns, and its arms terminated in long talons.

'We are doomed, Elric!' cried Yishana. She saw that the warriors were fleeing and she cried after them to come back. Elric stood there passively, knowing that alone he could not defeat the butterfly-creature.

'Best go with them, Yishana,' he mumured. 'I think it will be satisfied with me.'

'No!'

He ignored her and stepped towards the creature as it landed and began to glide over the ground in his direction. He drew a quiescent Stormbringer, which felt heavy in his hand. A little strength flowed into him, but not enough. His only hope was to strike a good blow at the creature's vitals and draw some of its own life-force into himself.

The creature's voice shrilled at him, and the strange, insane face twisted as he approached. Elric realised that this was no true supernatural denizen of the nether worlds, but a once-human creature warped by Theleb K'aarna's sorcery. At least it was mortal, and he had only physical strength to contend with. In better condition it would have been easy for him—but now . . .

The wings beat at the air as the taloned hands grasped at him. He took Stormbringer in both hands and swung the runeblade at the thing's neck. Swiftly the wings folded in to protect its neck and Stormbringer became entangled in the strange, sticky flesh. A talon caught Elric's arm, ripping it to the bone. He yelled in pain and yanked the sword from the enfolding wing.

He tried to steady himself for another blow, but the monster grabbed his wounded arm and began drawing him towards its now lowered head—and the horns that curled from it.

He struggled, hacking at the thing's arms with the extra strength that came with the threat of death.

Then he heard a cry from behind him and saw a figure from the corner of his eye, a figure that leapt forward with two

34

blades gleaming in either hand. The swords slashed at the talon's and with a shriek the creature turned on Elric's would-be rescuer.

It was Moonglum. Elric fell backwards, breathing hard, as he watched his little red-headed friend engage the monster.

But Moonglum would not survive for long, unless aided.

Elric racked his brain for some spell that would help; but he was too weak, even if he could think of one, to raise the energy necessary to summon supernatural help.

And then it came to him! Yishana! She was not as exhausted as he. But could she do it?

He turned as the air moaned to the beating of the creature's wings. Moonglum was only just managing to hold it off, his two swords flashing rapidly as he parried every effort to grasp him.

'Yishana!' croaked the albino.

She came up to him and placed a hand on his. 'We could leave, Elric—perhaps hide from that thing.'

'No. I must help Moonglum. Listen—you realise how desperate our position is, do you not? Then keep that in mind while you recite this rune with me. Perhaps together we may succeed. There are many kinds of lizards in these parts, are there not?'

'Aye—many.'

'Then this is what you must say—and remember that we shall all perish by Theleb K'aarna's servant if you are not successful.'

In the half worlds, where dwelt the master-types of all creatures other than Man, an entity stirred, hearing its name. The entity was called Haaashaastaak; and it was scaly and cold, with no true-intellect, such as men and gods possessed, but an *awareness,* which served it as well if not better. It was brother, on this plane, to such entities as Meerclar, Lord of the Cats, Roofdrak, Lord of the Dogs, Nuru-ah, Lord of the Cattle, and many, many others. This was Haaashaastaak, Lord of the Lizards. It did not really hear words in the exact sense, but it heard rhythms which meant much to it, even though it did not know why. The rhythms were being repeated over and over again, but seemed too faint to be worth much attention. It stirred and yawned, but did nothing . . .

35

> '*Haaashaastaak, Lord of Lizards,*
> *Your children were fathers of men,*
> *Haaashaastaak, Prince of Reptiles,*
> *Come aid a grandchild now!*
>
> '*Haaashaastaak, Father of Scales,*
> *Cold-blooded bringer of life . . .*'

It was a bizarre scene, with Elric and Yishana desperately chanting the rune over and over again as Moonglum fought on, slowly losing strength.

Haaashaastaak quivered and became more curious. The rhythms were no stronger, yet they seemed more insistent. He would travel, he decided, to that place where those he watched over dwelt. He knew that if he answered the rhythms, he would have to obey whatever source they had. He was not, of course, aware that such decisions had been implanted into him in a far distant age—the time before the creation of Earth, when the Lords of Law and Chaos, then inhabitants of a single realm and known by another name, had watched over the forming of things and laid down the manner and logic in which things should behave, following their great edict from the voice of the Cosmic Balance—the voice which had never spoken since.

Haaashaastaak betook himself, a little slothfully, to Earth.

Elric and Yishana were still chanting hoarsely, as Haaashaastaak made his sudden appearance. He had the look of a huge iguana, and his eyes were many-coloured, many faceted jewels, his scales seeming of gold, silver, and other rich metals. A slightly hazy outline surrounded him, as if he had brought part of his own environment with him.

Yishana gasped and Elric breathed a deep sigh. As a child he had learned the languages of all animal-masters, and now he must recall the simple language of the lizard-master, Haaashaastaak.

His need fired his brain, and the words came suddenly.

'*Haaashaastaak,*' he cried pointing at the butterfly-creature, '*mokik ankkuh!*'

The lizard lord turned its jewelled eyes on the creature and its great tongue suddenly shot out towards it, curling around the monster. It shrilled in terror as it was drawn towards the lizard lord's great maw. Legs and arms kicked as the mouth closed on it. Several gulps and Haaashaastaak had swallowed Theleb K'aarna's prize creation. Then it turned its head uncertainly about for a few moments and vanished.

Pain began to throb now through Elric's torn arm as Moonglum staggered towards him, grinning in relief.

'I followed behind you at a distance as you requested,' he said, 'since you suspected treachery from Theleb K'aarna. But than I spied the sorcerer coming this way and followed him to a cave in yonder hills,' he pointed. 'But when the deceased,' he laughed shakily, 'emerged from the cave, I decided that it would be best to chase *that*, for I had the feeling it was going in your direction.'

'I am glad you were so astute,' Elric said.

'It was your doing, really,' Moonglum replied. 'For, if you hadn't anticipated treachery from Theleb K'aarna, I might not have been here at the right moment.' Moonglum suddenly sank to the grass, leaned back, grinned, and fainted.

Elric felt very dazed himself. 'I do not think we need fear anything more from your sorcerer just yet, Yishana,' he said. 'Let us rest here and refresh ourselves. Perhaps then your cowardly soldiers will have returned, and we can send them to a village to get us some horses.'

They stretched out on the grass and, lying in each other's arms, went to sleep.

Elric was astonished to wake in a bed, a soft bed. He opened his eyes and saw Yishana and Moonglum smiling down at him.

'How long have I been here?'

'More than two days. You did not wake when the horses came, so we had the warriors construct a stretcher to bear you to Dhakos. You are in my palace.'

Elric cautiously moved his stiff, bandaged arm. It was still painful. 'Are my belongings still at the inn?'

'Perhaps, if they have not been stolen. Why?'

'I have a pouch of herbs there, which will heal this arm quickly and also supply me with a little strength, which I need badly.'

'I will go and see if they are still there,' Moonglum said and walked from the chamber.

Yishana stroked Elric's milk-white hair. 'I have much to thank you for, wolf,' said she. 'You have saved my kingdom—perhaps all the Young Kingdoms. In my eyes you are redeemed for my brother's death.'

'Oh, I thank you, madam,' said Elric with a mocking tone.

She laughed. 'You are still a Melnibonéan.'

'Still that, aye.'

'A strange mixture, however. Sensitive and cruel, sardonic and loyal to your little friend Moonglum. I look forward to knowing you better, my lord.'

'As to that, I am not sure if you will have the opportunity.'

She gave him a hard look. 'Why?'

'Your résumé of my character was incomplete, Queen Yishana—you should have added "careless of the world—and yet vengeful." I wish to be revenged on your pet wizard.'

'But he is spent, surely—you said so yourself.'

'I am, as you remarked, still a Melnibonéan! My arrogant blood calls vengeance on an upstart!'

'Forget Theleb K'aarna. I will have him hunted by my White Leopards. Even his sorcery will not win against such savages as they are!'

'Forget him? Oh, no!'

'Elric, Elric—I will give you my kingdom, declare you ruler of Jharkor, if you will let me be your consort.'

He reached out and stroked her bare arm with his good hand.

'You are unrealistic, queen. To take such an action would bring wholesale rebellion in your land. To your folk, I am still the Traitor of Imrryr.'

'Not now—now you are the Hero of Jharkor.'

'How so? They did not know of their peril and thus will feel no gratitude. It were best that I settled my debt with your wizard and went on my way. The streets must already be full of rumours that you have taken your brother's murderer to your bed. Your popularity with your subjects must be at its lowest, madam.'

'I do not care.'

'You will if your nobles lead the people in insurrection and crucify you naked in the city square.'

'You are familiar with our customs.'

'We Melnibonéans are a learned folk, queen.'

'Well versed in all the arts.'

'All of them.' Again he felt his blood race as she rose and barred the door. At that moment he felt no need for the herbs which Moonglum had gone to find.

When he tiptoed from the room that night, he found Moonglum waiting patiently in the antechamber. Moonglum proffered the pouch with a wink. But Elric's mood was not light. He took bunches of herbs from the pouch and selected what he needed.

Moonglum grimaced as he watched Elric chew and swallow the stuff. Then together they stole from the palace.

Armed with Stormbringer and mounted, Elric rode slightly behind his friend as Moonglum led the way towards the hills beyond Dhakos.

'If I know the sorcerers of Pan Tang,' murmured the albino, 'then Theleb K'aarna will be more exhausted than was I. With luck we will come upon him sleeping.'

'I shall wait outside the cave in that case,' said Moonglum, for he had experienced Elric's vengeance-taking in the past and did not relish watching Theleb K'aarna's slow death.

They galloped speedily until the hills were reached and Moonglum showed Elric the cave mouth.

Leaving his horse, the albino went soft-footed into the cave, his runesword ready.

Moonglum waited nervously for Theleb K'aarna's first shrieks, but none came. He waited until dawn began to bring the first faint light and then Elric, face dark with anger, emerged from the cave.

Savagely he grasped his horse's reins and swung himself into the saddle.

'Are you satisfied?' Moonglum asked tentatively.

'Satisfied, no! The dog has vanished!'

'Gone—but . . .'

'He was more cunning than I thought. There are several caves and I sought him in all of them. In the farthest I discovered traces of sorcerous runes on the walls and floor. He has transported himself somewhere and I could not discover where, in spite of deciphering most of the runes! Perhaps he went to Pan Tang.'

'Ah, then our quest has been futile. Let us return to Dhakos and enjoy a little more of Yishana's hospitality.'

'No—we go to Pan Tang.'

'But, Elric, Theleb K'aarna's brother sorcerers dwell there in strength; and Jagreen Lern, the theocrat, forbids visitors!'

'No matter. I wish to finish my business with Theleb K'aarna.'

'You have no proof that he is there!'

'*No matter!*'

And then Elric was spurring his horse away, riding like a man possessed or fleeing from dreadful peril—and perhaps he was both possessed and fleeing. Moonglum did not follow at once but thoughtfully watched his friend gallop off. Not normally introspective, he wondered if Yishana had not perhaps affected the albino more strongly than he would have wished. He did not think that vengeance on Theleb K'aarna was Elric's prime desire in refusing to return to Dhakos.

Then he shrugged and clapped his heels to his steed's flanks, racing to catch up with Elric as the cold dawn rose, wondering if they would continue towards Pan Tang once Dhakos was far enough behind.

But Elric's head contained no thoughts, only emotion flooded him—emotion he did not wish to analyse. His white hair streaming behind him, his dead-white, handsome face set his slender hands tightly clutching the stallion's reins, he rode. And only his strange, crimson eyes reflected the misery and conflict within him.

In Dhakos that morning, other eyes held misery, but not for too long. Yishana was a pragmatic queen.

From the glassless window of the stone tower it was possible to
see the wide river winding off between loose, brown banks,
through the heaped terrain of solid green copses which blended
very gradually into the mass of the forest proper. And out of
the forest, the cliff rose, grey and light-green, up and up, the
rock darkening, lichen-covered, to merge with the lower, and
even more massive, stones of the castle. It was the castle which
dominated the countryside in three directions, drawing the eye
from river, rock, or forest. Its walls were high and of thick
granite, with towers; a dense field of towers, grouped so as to
shadow one another.

Aubec of Malador marvelled and wondered how human
builders could ever have constructed it, save by sorcery. Brooding and mysterious, the castle seemed to have a defiant air, for
it stood on the very edge of the world.

At this moment the lowering sky cast a strange, deep-yellow
light against the western sides of the towers, intensifying the
blackness untouched by it. Huge billows of blue sky rent the
general racing greyness above, and mounds of red cloud crept
through to blend and produce more and subtler colourings.
Yet, though the sky was impressive, it could not take the gaze
away from the ponderous series of man-made crags that were
Castle Kaneloon.

Earl Aubec of Malador did not turn from the window until
it was completely dark outside; forest, cliff, and castle but
shadowy tones against the overall blackness. He passed a
heavy, knotted hand over his almost bald scalp and thoughtfully went towards the heap of straw which was his intended
bed.

The straw was piled in a niche created by a buttress and the
outer wall and the room was well-lighted by Malador's lantern.
But the air was cold as he lay down on the straw with his hand
close to the two-handed broadsword of prodigious size. This
was his only weapon. It looked as if it had been forged for a
giant—Malador was virtually that himself—with its wide

41

crosspiece and heavy, stone-encrusted hilt and five-foot blade, smooth and broad. Beside it was Malador's old, heavy armour, the casque balanced on top with its somewhat tattered black plumes waving slightly in a current of air from the window.

Malador slept.

His dreams, as usual, were turbulent; of mighty armies surging across blazing landscapes, curling banners bearing the blazons of a hundred nations, forests of shining lance-tips, seas of tossing helmets, the brave, wild blasts of the war-horns, the clatter of hooves, and the songs and cries and shouts of soldiers. These were dreams of earlier times, of his youth when, for Queen Eloarde of Lormyr, he had conquered all the Southern nations—almost to the edge of the world. Only Kaneloon, on the very edge, had he not conquered, and this because no army would follow him there.

For one of so martial an appearance, these dreams were surprisingly unwelcome, and Malador woke several times that night, shaking his head in an attempt to rid himself of them.

He would rather have dreamed of Eloarde, though she was the cause of his restlessness, but he saw nothing of her in his sleep; nothing of her soft, black hair that billowed around her pale face, nothing of her green eyes and red lips and her proud, disdainful posture. Eloarde had assigned him to this quest and he had not gone willingly, though he had no choice, for as well as his mistress she was also his Queen. The Champion was traditionally her lover—and it was unthinkable to Earl Aubec that any other condition should exist. It was his place, as Champion of Lormyr, to obey and go forth from her palace to seek Castle Kaneloon alone and conquer it and declare it part of her Empire, so that it could be said Queen Eloarde's domain stretched from the Dragon Sea to World's Edge.

Nothing lay beyond World's Edge—nothing save the swirling stuff of unformed Chaos which stretched away from the Cliffs of Kaneloon for eternity, roiling and broiling, multi-coloured, full of monstrous half-shapes—for Earth alone was Lawful and constituted of ordered matter, drifting in the sea of Chaos-stuff as it had done for aeons.

In the morning, Earl Aubec of Malador extinguished the lantern which he had allowed to remain alight, drew greaves and hauberk on to him, placed his black-plumed helm upon his head, put his broadsword over his shoulder and sallied out of the stone tower which was all that remained whole of some ancient edifice.

His leather-shod feet stumbled over stones that seemed partially dissolved, as if Chaos had once lapped here instead of against the towering Cliffs of Kaneloon. That, of course, was quite impossible, since Earth's boundaries were known to be constant.

Castle Kaneloon had seemed closer the night before and that, he now realised, was, because it was so huge. He followed the river, his feet sinking in the loamy soil, the great branches of the trees shading him from the increasingly hot sun as he made his way towards the cliffs. Kaneloon was now out of sight, high above him. Every so often he used his sword as an axe to clear his way through the places where the foliage was particularly thick.

He rested several times, drinking the cold water of the river and mopping his face and head. He was unhurried, he had no wish to visit Kaneloon, he resented the interruption to his life with Eloarde which he thought he had earned. Also he, too, had a superstitious dread of the mysterious castle, which was said to be inhabited only by one human occupant—the Dark Lady, a sorceress without mercy who commanded a legion of demons and other Chaos-creatures.

He regarded the cliffs at midday and regarded the path leading upward with a mixture of wariness and relief. He had expected to have to scale the cliffs. He was not one, however, to take a difficult route where an easy one presented itself, so he looped a cord around his sword and slung it over his back, since it was too long and cumbersome to carry at his side. Then, still in bad humour, he began to climb the twisting path.

The lichen-covered rocks were evidently ancient, contrary to the speculations of certain Lormyrian philosophers who asked why Kaneloon had only been heard of a few generations since. Malador believed in the general answer to this question—that explorers had never ventured this far until fairly recently. He glanced back down the path and saw the tops of the trees below him, their foliage moving slightly in the breeze. The tower in which he'd spent the night was just visible in the distance and, beyond that, he knew, there was no civilisation, no outpost of Man for many days' journey North, East, or West—can Chaos lay to the South? He had never been so close to the edge of the world before and wondered how the sight of unformed matter would affect his brain.

At length he clambered to the top of the cliff and stood, arms akimbo, staring up at Castle Kaneloon which soared a mile away, its highest towers hidden in the clouds, its immense walls rooted on the rock and stretching away, limited on both sides only by the edge of the cliff. And, on the other side of the cliff, Malador watched the churning, leaping Chaos-substance, predominantly grey, blue, brown, and yellow at this moment, though its colours changed constantly, spew like the sea-spray a few feet from the castle.

He became filled with a feeling of such indescribable profundity that he could only remain in this position for a long while, completely overwhelmed by a sense of his own insignificance. It came to him, eventually, that if anyone did dwell in the Castle Kaneloon, then they must have a robust mind or else must be insane, and then he sighed and strode on towards his goal, noting that the ground was perfectly flat, without blemish, green, obsidian, and reflecting imperfectly the dancing Chaos-stuff from which he averted his eyes as much as he could.

Kaneloon had many entrances, all dark and unwelcoming, and had they all not been of regular size and shape they might have been so many cave-mouths.

Malador paused before choosing which to take, and then walked with outward purposefulness towards one. He went into blackness which appeared to stretch away forever. It was cold; it was empty and he was alone.

He was soon lost. His footsteps made no echo, which was unexpected; then the blackness began to give way to a series of angular outlines, like the walls of a twisting corridor—walls which did not reach the unsensed roof, but ended several yards above his head. It was a labyrinth, a maze. He paused and looked back and saw with horror that the maze wound off in many directions, though he was sure he had followed a straight path from the outside.

For an instant, his mind became diffused and madness threatened to engulf him, but he battened it down, unslung his

44

sword, shivering. Which way? He pressed on, unable to tell, now, whether he went forward or backward.

The madness lurking in the depths of his brain filtered out and became fear and, immediately following the sensation of fear, came the shapes. Swift-moving shapes, darting from several different directions, gibbering, fiendish, utterly horrible.

One of these creatures leapt at him and he struck at it with his blade. It fled, but seemed unwounded. Another came and another and he forgot his panic as he smote around him, driving them back until all had fled. He paused and leaned, panting, on his sword. Then, as he stared around him, the fear began to flood back into him and more creatures appeared—creatures with wide, blazing eyes and clutching talons, creatures with malevolent faces, mocking him, creatures with half-familiar faces, some recognisable as those of old friends and relatives, yet twisted into horrific parodies. He screamed and ran at them, whirling his huge sword, slashing, hacking at them, rushing past one group to turn a bend in the labyrinth and encounter another.

Malicious laughter coursed through the twisting corridors, following him and preceding him as he ran. He stumbled and fell against a wall. At first the wall seemed of solid stone, then, slowly it became soft and he sank through it, his body lying half in one corridor, half in another. He hauled himself through, still on hands and knees, looked up and saw Eloarde, but an Eloarde whose face grew old as he watched.

'I am mad,' he thought. *'Is this reality or fantasy—or both?'* He reached out a hand, *'Eloarde!'*

She vanished but was replaced by a crowding horde of demons. He raised himself to his feet and flailed around him with his blade, but they skipped outside his range and he roared at them as he advanced. Momentarily, while he thus exerted himself, the fear left him again and, with the disappearance of the fear, so the visions vanished until he realised that the fear preceded the manifestations and he tried to control it.

He almost succeeded, forcing himself to relax, but it welled up again and the creatures bubbled out of the walls, their shrill voices full of malicious mirth.

This time he did not attack them with his sword, but stood his ground as calmly as he could and concentrated upon his

45

own mental condition. As he did so, the creatures began to fade away and then the walls of the labyrinth dissolved and it seemed to him that he stood in a peaceful valley, calm and idyllic. Yet, hovering close to his consciousness, he seemed to see the walls of the labyrinth faintly outlined, and disgusting shapes moving here and there along the many passages.

He realised that the vision of the valley was as much an illusion as the labyrinth and, with this conclusion, both valley and labyrinth faded and he stood in the enormous hall of a castle which could only be Kaneloon.

The hall was unoccupied, though well-furnished, and he could not see the source of the light, which was bright and even. He strode towards a table, on which were heaped scrolls, and his feet made a satisfying echo. Several great metal-studded doors led off from the hall, but for the moment he did not investigate them, intent on studying the scrolls and seeing if they could help him unravel Kaneloon's mystery.

He propped his sword against the table and took up the first scroll.

It was a beautiful thing of red vellum, but the black letters upon it meant nothing to him and he was astounded for, though dialects varied from place to place, there was only one language in all the lands of the Earth. Another scroll bore different symbols still, and a third he unrolled carried a series of highly stylised pictures which were repeated here and there so that he guessed they formed some kind of alphabet. Disgusted, he flung the scroll down, picked up his sword, drew an immense breath, and shouted:

'Who dwells here? Let them know that Aubec, Earl of Malador, Champion of Lormyr and Conqueror of the South claims this castle in the name of Queen Eloarde, Empress of all the Southlands!'

In shouting these familiar words, he felt somewhat more comfortable, but he received no reply. He lifted his casque a trifle and scratched his neck. Then he picked up his sword, balanced it over his shoulder, and made for the largest door.

Before he reached it, it sprang open and a huge, manlike thing with hands like grappling irons grinned at him.

He took a pace backward and then another until, seeing that the thing did not advance, stood his ground observing it.

It was a foot or so taller than he, with oval, multi-faceted

46

eyes that, by their nature, seemed blank. Its face was angular and had a grey, metallic sheen. Most of its body was comprised of burnished metal, jointed in the manner of armour. Upon its head was a tight-fitting hood, studded with brass. It had about it an air of tremendous and insensate power, though it did not move.

'A golem!' Malador exclaimed for it seemed to him that he remembered such man-made creatures from legends. 'What sorcery created *you*!'

The golem did not reply, but its hands—which were in reality comprised of four spikes of metal apiece—began slowly to flex themselves; and still the golem grinned.

This thing, Malador knew, did not have the same amorphous quality of his earlier visions. This was solid, this was real and strong, and even Malador's manly strength, however much he exerted it, could not defeat such a creature. Yet neither could he turn away.

With a scream of metal joints, the golem entered the hall and stretched its burnished hands towards the earl.

Malador could attack or flee, and fleeing would be senseless. He attacked.

His great sword clasped in both hands, he swung it sideways at the golem's torso, which seemed to be its weakest point. The golem lowered an arm and the sword shuddered against metal with a mighty clang that set the whole of Malador's body quaking. He stumbled backward. Remorselessly, the golem followed him.

Malador looked back and searched the hall in the hope of finding a weapon more powerful than his sword, but saw only shields of an ornamental kind upon the wall to his right. He turned and ran to the wall, wrenching one of the shields from its place and slipping it on to his arm. It was an oblong thing, very light, and comprising several layers of cross-grained wood. It was inadequate, but it made him feel a trifle better as he whirled again to face the golem.

The golem advanced, and Malador thought he noticed something familiar about it, just as the demons of the labyrinth had seemed familiar, but the impression was only vague. Kaneloon's weird sorcery was affecting his mind, he decided.

The creature raised the spikes on its right arm and aimed a swift blow at Malador's head. He avoided it, putting up his sword as protection. The spikes clashed against the sword and then the left arm pistoned forward, driving at Malador's stomach. The shield stopped this blow, though the spikes pierced it deeply. He yanked the buckler off the spikes, slashing at the golem's leg-joints as he did so.

Still staring into the middle-distance, with apparently no real interest in Malador, the golem advanced like a blind man as the earl turned and leapt on to the table, scattering the scrolls. Now he brought his huge sword down upon the golem's skull, and the brass studs sparked and the hood and head beneath it was dented. The golem staggered and then grasped the table, heaving it off the floor so that Malador was forced to leap to the ground. This time he made for the door and tugged at its latch-ring, but the door would not open.

His sword was chipped and blunted. He put his back to the door as the golem reached him and brought its metal hand down on the top edge of the shield. The shield shattered and a dreadful pain shot up Malador's arm. He lunged at the golem, but he was unused to handling the big sword in this manner and the stroke was clumsy.

Malador knew that he was doomed. Force and fighting skill were not enough against the golem's insensate strength. At the golem's next blow he swung aside, but was caught by one of its spike-fingers which ripped through his armour and drew blood, though at that moment he felt no pain.

He scrambled up, shaking away the grip and fragments of wood which remained of the shield, grasping his sword firmly. *'The soulless demon has no weak spot,'* he thought, *'and since it has no true intelligence, it cannot be appealed to. What would a golem fear?'*

The answer was simple. The golem would only fear something as strong or stronger than itself.

He must use cunning.

He ran for the upturned table with the golem after him, leaped over the table and wheeled as the golem stumbled but did not, as he'd hoped, fall. However, the golem was slowed by its encounter, and Aubec took advantage of this to rush for the door through which the golem had entered. It opened. He was in a twisting corridor, darkly shadowed, not unlike the labyrinth he had first found in Kaneloon. The door closed, but he could find nothing to bar it with. He ran up the corridor as the golem tore the door open and came lumbering swiftly after him.

The corridor writhed about in all directions, and, though he could not always see the golem, he could hear it and had the sickening fear that he would turn a corner at some stage and run straight into it. He did not—but he came to a door and, upon opening it and passing through it, found himself again in the hall of Castle Kaneloon.

He almost welcomed this familiar sight as he heard the golem, its metal parts screeching, continue to come after him. He needed another shield, but the part of the hall in which he now found himself had no wall-shields—only a large, round mirror of bright, clear-polished metal. It would be too heavy to be much use, but he seized it, tugging it from its hook. It fell with a clang and he hauled it up, dragging it with him as he stumbled away from the golem which had emerged into the room once more.

Using the chains by which the mirror had hung, he gripped it before him and, as the golem's speed increased and the monster rushed upon him, he raised this makeshift shield.

The golem shrieked.

Malador was astounded. The monster stopped dead and cowered away from the mirror. Malador pushed it towards the golem and the thing turned its back and fled, with a metallic howl, through the door it had entered by.

Relieved and puzzled, Malador sat down on the floor and studied the mirror. There was certainly nothing magical about it, though its quality was good. He grinned and said aloud:

'The creature *is* afraid of something. It is afraid of itself!'

He threw back his head and laughed loudly in his relief. Then he frowned. 'Now to find the sorcerers who created him and take vengeance on them!' He pushed himself to his feet, twisted the chains of the mirror more securely about his arm and went to another door, concerned lest the golem complete its circuit of the maze and return through the door. This door would not budge, so he lifted his sword and hacked at the latch for a few moments until it gave. He strode into a well-lit passage with what appeared to be another room at its far end—the door open.

A musky scent came to his nostrils as he progressed along

the passage—the scent that reminded him of Eloarde and the comforts of Lormyr.

When he reached the circular chamber, he saw that it was a bedroom—a woman's bedroom full of the perfume he had smelled in the passage. He controlled the direction his mind took, thought of loyalty and Lormyr, and went to another door which led off from the room. He lugged it open and discovered a stone staircase winding upward. This he mounted, passing windows that seemed glazed with emerald or ruby, beyond which shadow-shapes flickered so that he knew he was on the side of the castle overlooking Chaos.

The staircase seemed to lead up into a tower, and when he finally reached the small door at its top he was feeling out of breath and paused before entering. Then he pushed the door open and went in.

A huge window was set in one wall, a window of clear glass through which he could see the ominous stuff of Chaos leaping. A woman stood by this window as if awaiting him.

'You are indeed a champion, Earl Aubec,' said she with a smile that might have been ironic.

'How do you know my name?'

'No sorcery gave it me, Earl of Malador—you shouted it loudly enough when you first saw the hall in its true shape.'

'Was not *that*, then, sorcery,' he said ungraciously, 'the labyrinth, the demons—even the valley? Was not the golem made by sorcery? Is not this whole cursed castle of a sorcerous nature?'

She shrugged. 'Call it so if you'd rather not have the truth. Sorcery, in your mind at least, is a crude thing which only hints at the true powers existing in the universe.'

He did not reply, being somewhat impatient of such statements. He had learned, by observing the philosophers of Lormyr, that mysterious words often disguised commonplace things and ideas. Instead, he looked at her sulkily and over-frankly.

She was fair, with green-blue eyes and a light complexion. Her long robe was of a similar colour to her eyes. She was, in a secret sort of way, very beautiful and, like all the denizens of Kaneloon he'd encountered, a trifle familiar.

'You recognise Kaneloon?' she asked.

He dismissed her question. 'Enough of this—take me to the

masters of this place!'

'There is none but me, Micella the Dark Lady—and I am the mistress.'

He was disappointed. 'Was it just to meet you that I came through such perils?'

'It was—and greater perils even than you think, Earl Aubec. Those were not the monsters of your own imagination!'

'Taunt me not, lady.'

She laughed. 'I speak in good faith. The castle creates its defences out of your own mind. It is a rare man who can face and defeat his own imagination. Such a one has not found me here for two hundred years. All since have perished by fear—until now.'

She smiled at him. It was a warm smile.

'And what is the prize for so great a feat?' he said gruffly.

She laughed again and gestured towards the window which looked out upon the edge of the world and Chaos beyond. 'Out there nothing exists as yet. If you venture into it, you will be confronted again by creatures of your hidden fancy, for there is nothing else to behold.'

She gazed at him admiringly and he coughed in his embarrassment. 'Once in a while,' she said, 'there comes a man to Kaneloon who can withstand such an ordeal. Then may the frontiers of the world be extended, for when a man stands against Chaos it must recede and new lands spring into being!'

'So that is the fate you have in mind for me, sorceress!'

She glanced at him almost demurely. Her beauty seemed to increase as he looked at her. He clutched at the hilt of his sword, gripping it tight as she moved gracefully towards him and touched him, as if by accident. 'There is a reward for your courage.' She looked into his eyes and said no more of the reward, for it was clear what she offered. 'And after—do my bidding and go against Chaos.'

'Lady, know you not that ritual demands of Lormyr's Champion that he be the queen's faithful consort? I would not betray my word and trust!' He gave a hollow laugh. 'I came here to remove a menace to my queen's kingdom—not to be your lover and lackey!'

'There is no menace here.'

'That seems true . . .'

She stepped back as if appraising him anew. For her this was

51

unprecedented—never before had her offer been refused. She rather liked this solid man who also combined courage and imagination in his character. It was incredible, she thought, how in a few centuries such traditions could grow up—traditions which could bind a man to a woman he probably did not even love. She looked at him as he stood there, his body rigid, his manner nervous.

'Forget Lormry,' she said, 'think of the power you might have—the power of true creation!'

'Lady, I claim this castle of Lormyr. That is what I came to do and that is what I do now. If I leave here alive, I shall be judged the conqueror and you must comply.'

She hardly heard him. She was thinking of various plans to convince him that her cause was superior to his. Perhaps she could still seduce him? Or use some drug to bewitch him? No, he was too strong for either, she must think of some other stratagem.

She felt her breasts heaving involuntarily as she looked at him. She would have preferred to have seduced him. It had always been as much her reward as the heroes who had earlier won over the dangers of Kaneloon. And then, she thought, she knew what to say.

'Think, Earl Aubec,' she whispered. 'Think—new lands for your queen's Empire!'

He frowned.

'Why not extend the Empire's boundaries farther?' she continued. 'Why not *make* new territories?'

She watched him anxiously as he took off his helm and scratched his heavy, bald head. 'You have made a point at last,' he said dubiously.

'Think of the honours you would receive in Lormyr if you succeeded in winning not merely Kaneloon—but that which lies *beyond*!'

Now he rubbed is chin. 'Aye,' he said. 'Aye ...' His great brows frowned deeply.

'New plains, new mountains, new seas—new populations, even—whole cities full of people fresh-sprung and yet with the memory of generations of ancestors behind them! All this can be done by *you*, Earl of Malador—for Queen Eloarde and Lormyr!'

He smiled faintly, his imagination fired at last. 'Aye! If I

52

can defeat such dangers here—then I can do the same out there! It will be the greatest adventure in history! My name will become a legend—Malador, Master of Chaos!'

She gave him a tender look, though she had half-cheated him.

He swung his sword up on to his shoulder. 'I'll try this, lady.'

She and he stood together at the window, watching the Chaos-stuff whispering and rolling for eternity before them. To her it had never been wholly familiar, for it changed all the time. Now its tossing colours were predominantly red and black. Tendrils of mauve and orange spiralled out of this and writhed away.

Weird shapes flitted about in it, their outlines never clear, never quite recognisable.

He said to her: 'The Lords of Chaos rule this territory. What will they have to say?'

'They can say nothing, do little. Even they have to obey the Law of the Cosmic Balance which ordains that if man can stand against Chaos, then it shall be his to order and make Lawful. Thus the Earth grows, slowly.'

'How do I enter it?'

She took the opportunity to grasp his heavily muscled arm and point through the window. 'See—there—a causeway leads down from this tower to the cliff.' She glanced at him sharply. 'Do you see it?'

'Ah—yes—I had not, but now I do. Yes, a causeway.'

Standing behind him, she smiled a little to herself. 'I will remove the barrier,' she said.

He straightened his helm on his head. 'For Lormyr and Eloarde and only those do I embark upon this adventure.'

She moved towards the wall and raised the window. He did not look at her as he strode down the causeway into the multi-coloured mist.

As she watched him disappear, she smiled to herself. How easy it was to beguile the strongest man by pretending to go his way! He might add lands to his Empire, but he might find their populations unwilling to accept Eloarde as their Empress. In fact, if Aubec did his work well, then he would be creating more of a threat to Lormyr than ever Kaneloon had been.

Yet she admired him, she was attracted to him, perhaps,

because he was not so accessible, a little more than she had been to that earlier hero who had claimed Aubec's own land from Chaos barely two hundred years before. Oh, he had been a man! But he, like most before him, had needed no other persuasion than the allurement of her body.

Earl Aubec's weakness had lain in his strength, she thought. By now he had vanished into the heaving mists.

She felt a trifle sad that this time the execution of the task given her by the Lords of Law had not brought her the usual pleasure.

Yes perhaps, she thought, she felt a more subtle pleasure in his steadfastness and the means she had used to convince him.

For centuries had the Lords of Law entrusted her with Kaneloon and its secrets. But the progress was slow, for there were few heroes who could survive Kaneloon's dangers—few who could defeat self-created perils.

Yet, she decided with a slight smile on her lips, the task had its various rewards. She moved into another chamber to prepare for the transition of the castle to the new edge of the world.

THE GREAT CONQUEROR

CHAPTER ONE

He felt he was much more than one man. Not one god, even, but many ... There seemed to be a hundred other entities writhing within him. Writhing to release themselves. Every limb, every projection of bone seemed to be part of another being.

He lay on the fur-strewn bed, sweating, dominated by movement in his mind and body which he was incapable of controlling. Alexander the Great groaned in torment.

The buxom Corinthian woman spat into the rushes on the floor of the tavern.

'That for the God-King!'

But the silence around her put a stop to her enlarging the theme. The Thracian known as Simon of Byzantium lifted his bronze cup, the sleeve of his silk-trimmed jerkin falling back down his bronze arm, and sucked sweet Persian wine into his throat. He sensed the discomfort the other roisterers felt towards the woman and, because he could be cautious, dropped his arm from her thick waist and pushed her from him.

He looked down his long nose. His scarred face moved and he smiled as he addressed an old Persian soldier.

'You say you were in the army Darius led against Alexander?'

'That's right—a charioteer. His cavalry ran rings round us.'

'What did *you* think of him?'

'Alexander? I don't know. I was quite close to him at one stage and saw a spearman get a blow at him—struck him in the thigh. He yelled—not in pain but when he saw his own blood flowing. He couldn't believe it. For a short time he was an open target as he stared down at his thigh, dabbing at the blood with his finger and inspecting it. Then he shouted something— I didn't recognise the language—and was in command of himself again. They said the wound healed unnaturally quickly.'

'He claims to be the son of Zeus,' the Corinthian woman said from the shadows, 'but many Persians say he's evil Ahriman's spawn.'

Simon pursed his lips and fingered his wine cup. 'Perhaps he's just a mortal,' he suggested, 'a mortal of unusual vitality?'

'Perhaps,' the Persian soldier said. 'I only know he's conquered the world.'

'I heard he halted his Indian campaign at the River Indus—why should he do that?' Simon said.

'His Macedonians say they forced him to stop, but I cannot believe that. Even Alexander must tire—that's my theory. I think he needed to rest and recuperate. Throughout his campaigns he's hardly slept, must move on continually as if driven to conquer. Who knows what spurred him to conquest—or what made him put a temporary halt to his victories?'

'The Indians have an ancient and mighty religion of which we know little,' said a middle-aged and scrawny trader from Carthage. 'Could their Gods be stronger than ours? Stronger than Alexander?' He pulled at his grey-streaked beard. His many rings glinted in the ill-lit place.

'Such talk is heresy these days,' cautioned the Persian, but it could be seen that he was contemplating this idea.

'People talk of nothing but the Macedonian,' said the swarthy trader. 'From the Bosphorus to the Nile they curse or praise him. But what is he other than a man who has been lucky? Events have shaped him, not he them. He owes much to his foresighted father King Philip, and that warped mother Queen Olympias, both of whom, in their separate ways, prepared the world for his conquests. What reason for instance did he have for his meanderings in Persia some years ago? Why, instead of pressing on, did he embark on a wild goose chase after Darius? He had no reason save that events were not ready for him.'

'I like to think this of great men, also,' Simon smiled, 'but I would join his army for my own convenience.'

'So that's why you're in Babylon. I wondered about you, my friend. Where are you from?' The Carthaginian poured himself more wine from a skin.

'I was born in Thrace, but I'm Byzantine by adoption. I've

56

spent seven years there as Captain of Infantry. But now I've the urge to see the East and since Alexander goes East, decided to attach myself to his army. I hear he's in Babylon now?'

'That's true. But you might find him hard to meet—obviously he is not personally concerned with the hiring of mercenaries.' The Persian's tone was friendly.

'I've heard this man—or God—spoken of so often that I've a mind to meet him if that's possible.'

'Good luck to you, friend. He'll either kill you or promote you. He's a man of extremes.'

'Are not all great conquerors?'

'You're marvellous learned for a mercenary,' the Carthaginian grinned.

Simon picked up his scabbarded short-sword from the bench.

'And you're marvellous curious, friend. Know you not that all Arts are encouraged in Byzantium, just as they were in ancient Greece—including the Arts of Reading and Philosophy.'

The Persian laughed. 'That's the story Byzantium tells. I for one do not believe that any city could be so enlightened. All you Westerners yearn for a Greece that never was—your whole philosophy is based on a need for perfection; a perfection you can never attain because it never existed. Believe me, the gutters of Byzantium still stink!'

'Not so strongly as Persian jealousy,' Simon said, and left before he was called upon to take the argument to its conclusion.

But behind him in the tavern the Persian had not been angered. Instead he was laughing, wiping his mouth with his arm stump.

Simon heard the laughter as he crossed the dim Square of the Bazaar, almost deserted of merchants and customers. The sun was still setting. It was nearly curfew. A few merchants baling their goods looked up as he strode, a tall, gaunt, fighting man, in smooth old leather, towards the Street of the Bronzeworkers where he had a friend.

Around him, golden Babylon squatted like an ancient monster, containing all knowledge, all secrets, her stepped houses, palaces, and temples soaking the last of the sun into their burnished hides. He walked up the steeply rising street and came at length to a small white house without windows. He knocked.

For a while he waited patiently as darkness came. Eventually bolts were withdrawn on the other side of the door and it was opened. An eye gleamed. The door opened wider.

Wizened Hano smiled welcomingly. 'Come in, Simon. So you reached our splendid Babylon!'

Simon stepped into the house. It was very dark, over-hot, with the unpleasantly bitter smell of metal. The old Phoenician clutched at his arm and led him down the dark passage.

'Will you be staying in Babylon, my boy?' Hano said, and then, before Simon could answer this question: 'How's the sword?'

'I intend to see Alexander,' Simon said, disliking the old man's touch though he liked Hano greatly. 'And the sword is excellent, has kept its edge in a dozen fights—I intend to hire it to Alexander.'

Hano's grip tightened as they entered a dark, smoky room, a red brazier gleaming in its centre. Around the smoke-stained walls were weapons—swords, shields, lances—and several couches and small tables were scattered on the floor. The smoke caught in Simon's lungs and he coughed it out. Hano pointed to a couch. 'Sit down, Simon.' He shuffled towards his own couch on the other side of the brazier, stretched himself at full length and scratched his hooked nose.

'Alexander has many swords.'

'I know—but if you granted me a favour it might facilitate my meeting him.'

'I owe you friendship and more,' Hano said, 'for you saved me from an unpleasant death that time in Thebes nine years ago. But though I sense what you want of me I am reluctant to agree to it.'

'Why?'

'An old man's caution, maybe, but the stories I've been hearing of late have been disquieting. Alexander claims himself son of Zeus, Jupiter Ammon. Others say that the Persian evil one Ahriman possesses him. All or none of this may be true—but every oracle from here to Pela is prophesying turmoil and trouble for the world and the king who rules it. Perhaps you would be wiser to join some ordinary caravan travelling east?'

Hano pulled back his woollen robe, revealing a pale and unlovely leg. He poised his wrinkled hand and then almost hurled it at a spot on his leg and began to scratch at the place with his talons of nails.

'I'm sick of this prattle of gods and demons. Can no one be content simply to believe in men and what men could be if they ceased blaming their misfortunes on unseen gods rather than on their own ineffectiveness? Life's not easy, it is a hard task to live it well and with grace—but, by Hades, let's not complicate it with deities and water-nymphs!'

Simon spat into the brazier which flared and spluttered.

Hano scratched at his thigh, drawing back more of his robe to do so, revealing a greater expanse of unhealthy flesh.

'I have seen supernatural manifestations of evil, my boy.'

'You have seen what a muddled brain wished you to see.'

'What matter? Now, let's end this conversation before you yell more heresies and have us both arrested.'

'Heresy and treason combined if Alexander's chest-puffing claim be true.' Simon looked away from the old man's thin legs and stared into the brazier.

Hano changed the subject.

'In Utopia,' he said to Simon, 'you'd yet be seeking further perfection. You call yourself a realist, Simon—perfection is not a reality.'

'Realities can be created,' said Simon.

'True,' Hano agreed. 'But by the same logic, realities can be made unreal—unrealities made real. What if there *were* supernatural beings. How would you fit them into your theory?'

'The situation will never arise.'

'Let us hope so.'

The Phoenician turned his old twisted face towards Simon. The brazier light stained it a reddish brown, showing the wrinkles of mingled cynicism, fatalism, and good nature. Hano said at length: 'Very well.'

He got up and moved about the crowded room taking a pot from one shelf, a skin of wine from another.

Soon the smell of herbs came from the pot on the brazier as Hano brewed wine for his guest.

'You'll help,' Simon said.

'Alexander owes me a favour. But he has strange ways of

repaying debts and I'd not normally be foolish enough to remind him of this one.'

'What did you do for him?'

'Set the handle of a star-metal blade with black opals.'

'That was a favour!' Simon laughed.

Hano scowled, but genially. 'Know you not what that meant? It meant he could not directly handle iron or anything likely to conduct its force to his body. Black opal is one of the few gems which will serve to negate the flow.'

'So?'

'So Alexander has a weakness. Iron will harm him.'

'If I had such a secret I would kill the man who held it.' Simon said reflectively.

'Not if you were Alexander and the man was dear to Olympias.'

'*You* know Queen Olympias!'

'Olympias wishes me kept alive so I can feed her with secrets.'

'Dark secrets, I'll warrant, if the stories of her are half-true.'

'They do not touch the real truth about her.'

'Does she really sport with snakes at these rites?'

'Aye—and black goats are present too.'

Simon swore.

Hano handed him a cup of hot wine. As he drank he said: 'I'm impatient to meet the God-King—how will you help?'

'I'll give you a letter and a token to take to Alexander. But be wary, my boy. Be wary.'

CHAPTER TWO

Though he rarely admitted it, the idea of a supernatural world of gods and spirits disturbed Simon. Had it been practicable he might have become a militant atheist but instead he kept his opinions secret for the most part and did his utmost not to question them or even think of them.

When he reached the great golden palace of Alexander he paused and stared up at it with admiration. It was illuminated by hundreds of torches many of which, on long poles, surrounded the palace. Others flared on its many ramparts.

Two guards came forward. They were Babylonians in high helmets with oiled hair and beards. Their javelins threatened him.

In poor Babylonian Simon said:

'I come to see King Alexander—I have a token and a letter for him.'

They treated him with some respect, though they divested him of his sword and led him to the main gate where, after conversation he was admitted.

He was made to wait several times, being studied and questioned by a variety of viziers and minions of the king, but at last he was ushered into a large chamber.

Big windows let in the flickering torchlight. A great bed of brass, silver, and gold, heaped with silks and furs, was in the centre of the room.

Alexander was sitting up in bed. He had been sweating, Simon could see. His nose told him the same story.

The odour, in fact was bad. Far worse than ordinary perspiration. Simon couldn't place the smell.

With a degree of nervousness Simon approached the huge bed.

Suddenly, King Alexander grinned and stuck out a handsome hand.

'You have a letter for me, I hear—and a token?'

'I have, sire.' Simon gave the letter and the little talisman to Alexander, studying the king's strange face. In a way it was boyish, in another ancient and sensuous. He had a long nose and thick lips, heavily-lidded eyes, and brown, curly hair. Simon was taken aback by the king's lack of ceremony, by his friendly grin. Was this the God-King? The spawn of evil?

Alexander read the letter quickly, nodding to himself.

'Did Hano tell you of my debt to him?'

'No, sire,' Simon said tactfully.

'He has many secrets, Hano—but he's an old man and, in his generosity, keeps few to himself I've heard.'

'He seems curiously tight-lipped, sire,' Simon replied, anxious for his friend's life. 'and even I who saved his life one time in Thebes can never get a full reply to any question I ask him.'

Alexander looked up sharply, staring Simon in the face with

61

peculiarly wide eyes.

'So you wish to join my army. Hano recommends you as a fighting man—suggests you join my staff. I choose my officers with care, Simon of Byzantium.'

'I wish only a trial, sire.'

'You shall have it.'

Alexander studied the letter again.

'You're from Byzantium, I note. My father Philip was repulsed by that city some years ago—but that does not mean I can have no love for the city—perhaps the contrary. It's well known I disliked him and can admire a city which withstood his attack.' Alexander smiled again, 'Though she did not hold out for long against Philip's son, did she?'

'No, sire.'

Alexander had an almost tangible vitality, but he was evidently unwell. This ailment was not solely confined to his body, either, Simon felt.

Alexander mused, caressing the little amulet.

'I have need of a herald—a man who can travel between wherever I am campaigning and the capital of Macedonia.'

'I thought Persia was your base these days, sire.'

'You've been listening to Greek and Macedonian criticism, no doubt. They say I've forsaken my own lands for the flesh-pots and honours of the east. That's a lie. It is too far to travel back always to Pela. Persia offers a better base for my operations. There are still a few acres of the world left for me to conquer, Simon—and they all lie Eastwards.'

Alexander sank back into his silks, eyeing the Thracian.

'You'll serve my mother and myself as a messenger.'

Simon put his hand to his lips and said courteously: 'I had rather hoped to go with the army, sire.'

Alexander frowned slightly. 'And so you will, of course. No doubt there'll be fighting for you—and new knowledge. I'm pleased that you're literate. Most of my captains are chosen for several qualities—courage, loyalty—and learning. You appear to have courage and learning—but I must find out about your loyalty, you understand.'

Simon nodded. 'That is logical, sire.'

'Good, then——' Alexander broke off as the doors of the chamber opened behind Simon. The Thracian turned to stare

62

at the door.

A vizier, in long cloth-of-gold robes, hurried into the room. He prostrated himself before the king's bed.

'Son of Zeus,' he mumbled, 'a message.'

'Is it secret?'

'No, sire—they say it is already common knowledge.'

'Then speak—what is it?' Alexander propped himself into a sitting position again.

'A massacre, sire—in Lonarten—a troop of your Macedonian horse went berserk, killed many hundreds of women and children. There are rumours of cannibalism and unhealthy rites...' the vizier stopped as a smile crossed Alexander's sensuous lips. 'The people are asking for your interference—for compensation.'

Alexander smiled again. Simon was sickened by the sight. The king could be seen to grip hold of the bed-clothes as if attempting to control himself. He groaned once, slightly.

With effort he said: 'We must call a halt to—we must stop...' Then he flung back his handsome head and bellowed with laughter. It was a laughter totally evil, a horrible, malicious joy which seethed around the room, echoing and roaring in Simon's horrified ears.

'Seize the complainers,' Alexander shouted, 'we'll sell them as eunuchs to the harems of Turkey. Teach them that the ways of a god are not the ways of a mere king—teach them not to question the word or actions of the Son of Zeus!'

Hurriedly, the vizier backed out of the room.

Simon, forgetful for his own safety, leaned forward and shouted into Alexander's twisted face:

'You are mad—for your own sake do not let this massacre continue. Your unruly troops will cause a revolution—you will lose your empire.'

Alexander's eyes opened even wider. A hand leapt from the silks and furs and seized Simon's ear. The mouth curled and even teeth moved as Alexander snarled:

'For you I will *invent* a death!'

Simon grasped the wrist attempting to wrest himself from Alexander's grip. He was sickened, trembling and shaken by the strength in one so evidently ill. He felt the presence of some-

63

thing more than common insanity. What had changed the pleasant, practical soldier into this manifestation of evil? How could such different qualities exit in one body? Terror clouded his mind.

With a wrench he was free of the king's grasp and backed panting away from him.

'They said you were Ahriman's spawn—and I did not believe them,' he gasped.

Alexander grimaced, flung back the bed-clothes and leapt to the ground, advancing towards Simon, hands outstretched.

'I am Zeus's son—born of god and mortal to rule the world. Abase yourself, heretic, for I have the power to send you to Hades!'

'All men have that power,' Simon said, turned and ran for the great doors, tugged them open and, before he could be stopped fled down the shouting corridors, blind to everything but the need to escape from the screaming madman behind him.

He remembered little of the flight, of the two fights, in the first of which he somehow gained a weapon, of his breathless running through the streets of Babylon with hordes of soldiers seeking him out.

He ran.

He had run himself virtually to death when several warriors pinned him in a blind alley and he turned, snarling like an animal to defend himself. Crouching, sword raised, he waited for them as they cautiously advanced.

They had not expected such ferocity. He had cut the first soldier down in a trice and sliced the flesh from another's arm.

In front of him, as if superimposed on the real scene before him, was the great, sensuous head of Alexander still roaring with crazy laughter.

Simon had seen madmen many times. But Alexander had more than madness. He slashed with his sword and missed his target, fell forward, rolled on his back, brought his sword across his face to deflect a blade which had hurtled down through the confused night. He edged back, flung himself sideways, slashing, scrambled up and brought the edge of his sword up to chop a man's jugular.

Then he was running again, every limb aching, but a terrible fear, a fear of more than death or torture, driving, driving him onward to escape.

When the silent, dark-robed men appeared out of the night and surrounded them he cut at one but his sword seemed to meet metal, his hand went numb and the blade fell to the stones of the streets.

Alexander's face rose before him, laughing, laughing. The roaring, evil merriment filled his head, then his whole body until it seemed that he, Simon, was Alexander, that he was enjoying the bloody joke, the evil, malignant glee pouring wildly from his shaking body.

Then peace of a kind and hazy, mysterious dreams where he saw strange shapes moving through the smoke from a million red and glowing braziers.

Simon felt a hard, smooth surface beneath his back.

He opened his eyes warily.

A lean, white, thin-lipped face looked kindly down at him.

'I am Abaris,' he said.

'Simon of Byzantium,' said the Thracian.

'You have witnessed darkness?' It was only half a question.

'Yes,' Simon replied, bemused.

'We are men of light. The Magi welcome you. You are safe here.'

'Magi? They are priests in Persia—but you're no Persian.'

'That is so.'

'Abaris? There is an Abaris of legend—a wizard, was he not—a priest of Apollo who rode on an arrow?'

The Magi made no reply to this, simply smiled.

'You have incurred the wrath of Alexander. How long would you say you had to live?'

'A strange question. I'd say as long as my wits were sharp enough to evade the searchings of his soldiers.'

'You would be wrong.'

Simon pushed himself upright on the wide bench and looked around him. Two other priests sat regarding him from across the bare room. Daylight filtered in from a hole in the ceiling.

'Do I really owe you my life?'

'We think you do—but you are in no debt. We wish we could give such concrete aid to all enemies of Alexander.'

'I am not his enemy—he is mine.'

'You have witnessed what he is—can you still say that?'

Simon nodded. 'I am his enemy,' he agreed and then amended this with: 'Or at least the enemy of what he represents.'

'You are exact—we also are the enemies of what Alexander represents.'

Simon put his head on one side and smiled slightly. 'Ah—let us be careful. He is insane, that is all. He represents material evil, not supernatural.'

Briefly, Abaris looked impatiently away, frowning. Then his features resumed their earlier look.

'It is a bold thing to be an unbeliever in these times.'

'Bold or not—it is what I am.' Simon swung his legs off the bench. He felt incredibly weak.

Abaris said: 'We Magi worship Ormuzd. Simply—Alexander represents Ahriman.'

'These are the twin facets of your single deity are they not?' Simon said. He nodded. 'I know a little about your cult—it's cleaner than most. You worship Fire, Sun, and Light—with a minimum of ritual.'

'True. A man who is confident in his soul needs little ritual.'

Simon was satisfied by this.

'We would be grateful if you would ally yourself with us, the Magi,' Abaris said quietly. 'In return we will protect you from Alexander's minions as best we can.'

'I told you—and I do not wish to seem ungrateful—my wits will keep me safe from the Macedonian's warriors.'

'We refer to his supernatural minions.'

Simon shook his head. 'I respect your beliefs—but I cannot accept them personally.'

Abaris leaned forward and said urgently, softly:

'Simon, you must aid us. Alexander and his mother are both possessed. For years we have been aware of this. For years we have attempted to fight the forces possessing them—and we are losing. You have seen how Ahriman controls Alexander. You must aid us!'

Simon said: 'You have cloaked the simple fact of Alexander's madness in a shroud of supernatural speculation.'

Abaris shook his head, saying nothing. Simon continued:

66

'I have seen many men go mad with riches and power—Alexander is another. When he dies his good works will survive but the evil will be eliminated by time.'

'You are naïve, young man. Why, Achilles believed that ...' Abaris bit his lip and lapsed into silence.

'Achilles? He died a thousand years ago. How do you know what he believed?'

Abaris turned away. 'Of course, I could not know,' he said. His eyes were hooded.

'You give me cause to think you really are the Abaris of legend,' Simon smiled. He was joking. But even to his ears the joke rang true.

Abaris said: 'Can a man live for more than a thousand years?'

'No,' Simon said, 'no.' He said it almost savagely, for it was what he wished to believe.

Out there, in a palace of Babylon, there was *evil*, he thought. But it was not, could not be—*must* not be supernatural.

Abaris now said:

'Alexander has reigned almost thirteen years—a mystic number. Our oracles prophesied that the turning point would come after thirteen years of rule. Now, as we fear, Alexander and the forces which act through him will bring an unchecked reign of evil to the world—or else, and the chance is small, he will be stopped.'

'You wish me to aid you in this. I must dissent. To help you I would have to believe you—that I cannot do.'

Abaris seemed to accept this. When he next spoke it was in a detached, trancelike voice.

'Ahriman—the multiplicity of Ahrimans whom we designate by the one name—selected Olympias many years ago. He needed a vessel through which to work and, at that time, no mortal had been born who would serve Ahriman's purpose. So he took possession of poor Olympias. Philip, that great and wronged man, went regularly to the Isle of Samothrace on pilgrimage and, one year, Olympias made it her business to be there also. A love potion was all she needed. Philip was enamoured of her. They had a son—Alexander ...'

Simon said wearily: 'This is mere gossip such as old women make in the markets.'

'Ormuzd protect you if you ever learn the truth,' was all Abaris said.

Simon rose shakily. 'If there is anything I can do to repay you—some material act, perhaps—I am very willing.'

Abaris thought for a moment. Then he took a scroll from his robe. He unrolled it and glanced over the weird script. It was not Persian, Simon knew, but what it was he could not tell.

Abaris handed the scroll to Simon. 'We'll furnish you with a horse and a disguise. Will you go to Pela for us? Will you deliver a message to our brothers?'

'Willingly,' Simon said, though he was aware that to journey to the capital of Macedonia would be courting danger.

'They live in secret,' Abaris told Simon, 'but we will tell you how to find them. Also we will furnish you with weapons, a horse and a disguise of some sort.'

'I'd be grateful for that,' Simon smiled.

'We'll give you a day for resting and allowing the herbs we'll give you to drink to do their work—then you can start off. You should have little trouble here, for our magic will protect you and we know a secret way out of the city.'

Simon lay back on the bench. 'Healing herbs will be very welcome,' he said, 'and something to help me take a dreamless sleep . . .'

CHAPTER THREE

Outside, the courtiers glanced at one another, not daring to enter the room where a man groaned.

A short, clever-looking man in ornate war-gear turned to a calm-faced, sensitive man.

'Why was he so anxious to apprehend the Thracian, I wonder, Anaxarchus?'

The sensitive man shook his head. 'I have no idea. I hear he was from my home city, Abdera, before he went to Byzantium. For all people say that the folk of Abdera are stupid, some very clever men were born there.'

'And you, of course, are one,' the soldier smiled ironically.

68

'I must be—I am philosopher attached to Alexander's train,' Anaxarchus said.

The warrior took several nervous paces up the corridor, wheeled around, cursing. 'By the Salamander's breath, are we never to finish our conquests? What is wrong with Alexander, Anaxarchus? How long has he been like this? Rumours came to Egypt, but I discounted them.'

'He is ill, Ptolemy, that is all,' Anaxarchus said, but he did not believe his own words.

'That is *all*! Even if I had not heard the Oracle of Libya speak of terrible strifings in this world and the others I would be troubled. Things are happening. Anaxarchus—doom-clouds are covering the world.'

'Gloomy, Ptolemy—he is only sick. He has a fever.'

Another awful groan came from behind the doors, a terrified and terrible groan of awful agony. Neither did it seem to represent physical pain but some deeper agony of spirit.

'An unusual fever,' Ptolemy said savagely. He strode towards the doors, but Anaxarchus blocked his passage.

'No, Ptolemy—you would not emerge with your sanity intact, I warn you.'

Ptolemy looked at the scholar for a moment, then turned and almost ran down the corridor.

Inside the locked room, the man—or god—groaned terribly. It was as if the bones of his face were breaking apart to form individual beings. What was he? Even he could not be sure. For years he had been certain of his own power, confident that his greatness was his own. But now, it was obvious to him, poor, tormented Alexander, that he was nothing—nothing but a vessel, an agent through which many forces worked—and even those forces were untied under a common name. He knew then, also that they had entered many others in the past that, if his strength broke, they would enter many more until their work was done.

Part of him begged for death.

Part of him attempted to fight that which was in him.

Part of him planned—crime.

Simon cloaked and armed, clamped his knees against his steed's back and galloped over the sparsely-covered plains of

Babylon, the folds of his cloak flying behind him like the wings of a diving bat.

The horse snorted, its sturdy legs flashing, its eyes big and its heart pounding.

For two hours, Simon had ridden in safety.

But now the cold night air above him was alive with dreadful sounds.

He drew his sword from its scabbard and rode on, telling himself that the noises were the flapping wings of vultures.

Then a shape came swooping in front of him. He caught a glimpse of a pale, human face. But it was not entirely human. Snakes twined on its head, blood dripped from its eyes. The horse came to a sudden halt, reared whinnying.

Simon closed his eyes against the sight.

'The herbs the Magi gave me have induced visions,' he told himself aloud in shaking tones.

But he could not believe it. He had seen them.

The Eumenides—the Furies of legend!

For the face had been that of a woman.

Now the sounds came closer, ominous. Simon urged the frightened horse onwards. Sharp female faces with serpents in place of hair, blood streaming from malevolent eyes, hands like talons, swooped and cackled about him. It was nightmare.

Then, quite suddenly, there came a dull booming sound from the distance, like the far away sound of surf. Nearer and nearer it came until the night opened to brightness, a strange golden light which seemed to break through the blackness, splintering it into fragments. The winged creatures were caught in the glare, wheeled about uncertainly, shrieking and keening.

They were gone.

The light faded.

Simon rode on. And still he insisted to himself that what he had witnessed was hallucination. Something done to his weary brain by the potion the Magi had given him.

The rest of the night was full of nauseous sound, glimpses of things which flew or wriggled. But, convinced that he dreamed, horrified yet keeping close hold on sanity, Simon pushed the steed onwards towards Pela.

Horse and man rested for only a few hours at a time. The journey took days until, at length, eyes sunken in his head from tiredness, face grey and gaunt and mind numb he arrived at the Macedonian capital and sought out the Magi in the clay-built slums of the city.

Massiva, head of the secret order in Pela, was a tall, handsome Numidian. He greeted Simon warmly.

'We were informed of your coming and did our best, when you came close enough, to ward off the dangers which Alexander's minions sent against you.'

Simon did not reply to this. Silently, he handed over the scroll.

Massiva opened it, read it, frowning.

'This we did not know,' he said. 'Olympias has sent aid to Alexander in Babylon.'

The priest offered no explanation, so Simon did not ask for one.

Massiva shook his head wearily. 'I do not understand how one human can endure so much,' he said, 'but then she has other aid than human . . .'

'What are these stories about her?' Simon asked, thinking that he might at last find some truth where before he had heard nothing but rumour and hints.

'The simple facts concerning her activities are common knowledge here,' Massiva told him. 'She is an ardent initiate of a number of mystery cults, all worshipping the dark forces. The usual unpleasant rites, secret initiations, orgiastic celebrations. Three of the main ones, supposedly having no communication with one another, are the cults of Orpheus, Dionysius and Demeter. It's hinted that Alexander was conceived at one of these rites. In a way that is the truth—for Olympias was selected by the Dark One when she was a girl participating in the rites of a similar cult.'

Simon shook his head impatiently at this. 'I asked you for facts—not speculation.'

Massiva looked surprised. 'I indulged in no speculation, my friend. Why, the whole city lives in fear of Olympias and her friends and servants. Evil is so thick here that ordinary folk can hardly breathe for its stink.'

Simon said shortly: 'Well, I hope the information is useful to you. I've paid my debt, at least. Now, can you recommend a tavern where I can stay?'

71

'I can recommend none well, in this cursed city. You might try the *Tower of Cimbri*. It's comfortable, so I've heard. But be wary, take iron to bed with you.'

'I'd do that in any event,' Simon grinned, 'with Alexander after my blood and me staying in his home city.'

'You're courageous, Thracian—do not be foolish.'

'Don't worry, friend.' Simon left the house, remounted his horse and rode it towards the tavern quarter, eventually locating the *Tower of Cimbri*.

He was about to enter when he heard the sound of running from an alley which ran along the side of the building. Then a girl screamed. Drawing his sword he ran into the alley and, because he had become so hardened to sights of horror hardly noticed the misshapen creatures menacing a frightened girl, save that they were armed and evidently powerful. The girl's eyes were round with fear and she was half-fainting. One of the twisted men put out a blunt paw to seize her, but wailed out its pain as Simon's sword caught it in the shoulder blades.

The others turned, reaching for their weapons. Simon cut two down before they could draw their swords. The fourth swung at Simon but was too clumsy. He died in a moment, his neck cloven.

Instead of thanking him, the girl stared down at the corpses in terror.

'You fool,' she muttered.

'Fool?' Simon was taken aback.

'You have killed four of Queen Olympias's retainers—did you not recognise the livery—or their kind?'

'I'm a stranger in Pela.'

'Then leave now—or be doomed.'

'No, I must see that you are safe. Quickly—I have a horse waiting in the street.' He supported her with one arm though she protested and helped her into the saddle.

He got up behind her.

'Where do you live?'

'Near the west wall—but hurry, be Hera, or they'll find the corpses and give chase.'

Following her directions, Simon guided the horse through the evening half-light.

They came to a pleasant, large house, surrounded by a

72

garden which in turn was enclosed in high walls. They rode through the gate and she dismounted, closing them behind her. An old man appeared in the doorway to the courtyard.

'Camilla? What's happening?'

'Later, father. Have the servants stable the horse and make sure all the gates are locked—Olympias's retainers attempted to kidnap me again. This man saved me from them—but four are dead.'

'Dead? Gods!' The old man pursed his lips. He was dressed in a loose toga and had a stern, patrician face. He was evidently a nobleman, though his black-haired daughter was most unlike him.

Quickly, Simon was ushered into the house. Servants were summoned bringing bread, cheese, and fruit. He ate gratefully. As he ate he told as much of his personal story as he wished to divulge. The patrician, Merates, listened without commenting.

When Simon had finished, Merates made no direct remark but instead said, half to himself:

'If King Philip had not continued his line, there would be peace and achievement in this war-wrecked world. I curse the name of Alexander—and the she-snake who bore him. If Alexander had been left to his father's teaching, he might well have carried on the great plan of Philip. But his warped mother put different ideas into his head—turned him against his father. Now there is evil on every wind, it blows east and west, south and north—and the hounds of darkness rend, slaver, and howl in Alexander's bloody wake.'

Camilla shuddered. She had changed her street robe into a loose, diaphanous gown of blue silk. Her long, black, unbound hair fell down her back, gleaming like dark wine.

She said: 'Now, though Alexander's off on his conquests, Olympias terrorises Pela more than ever before. All comely youths and girls are sought out to take part in her ghastly rituals. For ten or more months she has tried to encourage me to join until, at last, her patience failed and she attempted to kidnap me. She will know that someone killed the servitors—but she need not know it was you, Simon.'

Simon nodded mutely. He found it difficult to speak as he breathed in the girl's dark beauty, intoxicated by it as he had never before been.

73

They were troubled times. Times of high deeds and feats of learning; times of obscene evil and wild daring. Alexander mirrored his times. With one breath he would order a massacre, with another honour a conquered city for its courage in withstanding him. His great horse Bucephalus bore his bright armoured master across the known world. Fire destroyed ancient seats of civilisation, wise men were slain and innocents drowned in the flood tide of his conquests. Yet he caused new cities to be raised and libraries to be built. Men of learning followed in his train—this pupil of Aristotle—and he was an enigma to all. Greece, Persia, Babylonia, Assyria, Egypt, all fell to him. Four mighty races, four ancient civilisations bore Alexander's yoke. People had speculated on whether he was a force for darkness or enlightenment—whether he would rend the world to fragments or unite it in lasting peace. An enigma.

But now the year was 323 B.C. and Alexander was aged 32. He had ruled over twelve years—soon he would have reigned thirteen . . .

In the dark caverns of creation, existing within a multiplicity of dimensions, vital evil thrived, chuckling and plotting—crime.

For thirteen years had the forces of Light and Darkness warred in poor Alexander's soul and body, unbeknownst to the proud, grandiose and arrogant world-conqueror. But now the stars proclaimed that a certain time had come.

And Alexander suffered . . .

Riders galloped towards the corners of the world. Bright banners whipped in the wind as armies sped across the lands around the Mediterranean. Ships groaned with the weight of armoured soldiers. Blood flowed like wine and wine like water. Corpses roasted in guttering castles and the earth shook to the coming of Alexander's cavalry.

And now messengers rode to the camps of his captains, recalling them. They were needed. The final conquest was to be made. But it would not be Alexander's triumph. The triumph would belong to a greater conqueror. Some called him Ahriman.

Hastily now Alexander's captains mounted their chariots and headed towards Babylon. Many had to cross oceans, continents.

Every oracle prophesied doom—some said for Alexander,

74

some said for the world. Never, they said, had evil clouded the world as much as now.

Ahriman had prepared the world through Alexander.

Soon the Powers of Light would be destroyed for ever and, though it might take many more centuries of completion, Ahriman could begin his plans of conquest and, finally, destruction.

There were more vehicles for his plans.

CHAPTER FOUR

Simon lazed back on a bench and ran his hand over Camilla's warm shoulders.

'Do not the heroes of legend always claim such reward from the maidens they rescue?' he asked mockingly.

She smiled at him affectionately.

'The Camilla of legend, if you remember, had nought to do with men. I've a mind to emulate her.'

'A sad waste.'

'For you, perhaps, but not for me . . .'

Simon pretended to sigh. 'Very well,' he said, 'I can see I shall have to wait until you eventually succumb to my undouted attraction.'

Again she smiled. 'You have been here a week and I have not fallen yet.'

'It was good of your father to give me the position of Captain of his Bodyguard, particularly since he is risking arrest if Olympias should ever discover that I slew her servants.'

'Merates is a good and wise man,' Camilla said seriously, 'one of the few left in Pela, these days. He was close to Philip and admired him greatly. But Philip's son would have nothing to do with his father's councillors so now Merates lives in quiet retirement.'

Simon had already learnt that Camilla was the foster daughter of Merates, that she had been born to a loved and trusted Paeonian slave who had died when she was a child.

He had grown to respect the old nobleman and planned,

though it was dangerous for him, to stay in Pela and probably settle there. He had already fallen in love with Camilla.

And so he courted her and although she gave him no reason to cease this courtship, on the other hand she did not encourage him overmuch. She knew him for a soldier-of-fortune and a wanderer. Perhaps she wanted to be certain of him.

But they were dark times and Simon, rationalist though he was, could not be unaware of them. He sensed the gathering storm and was restless.

One day as he was instructing a group of slaves in the art of using the shield, Merates came hurrying into the courtyard.

'Simon—a word with you.'

The Thracian propped his sword against the wall and went with Merates into the house.

There were tears in Merates's eyes when he spoke.

'Camilla is gone. She had to go on an errand in the market—a regular monthly visit to settle our score with the merchants with whom we trade. She has been gone four hours—she is normally gone one . . .'

Simon's body grew taut. 'Olympias? Do you think . . . ?'

Merates nodded.

Simon turned, went swiftly to his quarters where he buckled on his leather belt bearing the scabbarded sword the Magi had given him.

He flung a blanket over his horse's back, rode it from the stable, ducking his head beneath the door beam, through the gates of the house and down the streets of Pela to the city centre.

He enquired in the market for her. She had not been seen there for well over two hours. Thinking swiftly, he headed for the slums of the city, dismounted outside a certain door and knocked.

Massiva, the black Numidian priest answered the door himself. He was dressed like a slave—evidently disguised.

'Come in, Simon. It is good to see you.'

'I wish aid, Massiva. And in return I may be able to help you.'

Massiva ushered him inside.

'What is it?'

'I am certain that Queen Olympias has kidnapped Camilla,

76

Lord Merates's daughter.'

Massiva's expression did not change. 'It is likely—Camilla is reputed beautiful and a virgin. Olympias seeks such qualities. Either she will corrupt Camilla and force her to take an active part in the rites—or else she will make her take a passive part.'

'Passive? What do you mean?'

'The blood of virgins is needed in several spells.'

Simon shuddered.

'Can you help me? Tell me where I may find her!'

'The Rites of Cottyttia begin tonight. That is where to look.'

'Where do they take place?'

'Come, I will draw you a map. You will most likely perish in this, Simon. But you will be convinced that we have spoken truth in the past.'

Simon looked at the Negro sharply. Massiva's face was expressionless.

They called her Cotys and she was worshipped as a goddess in Thrace, Macedonia, Athens, and Corinth. For centuries her name had been connected with licentious revelry—but never had she prospered so well than in Pela where Queen Olympias danced with snakes in her honour. Though only part of a greater Evil One, she flourished and grew on the tormented souls of her acolytes and their victims.

The house stood on its own on a hill.

Simon recognised it from Massiva's description. It was night, silver with rime and moonlight, but there were movements in the shadows and shapes of evil portent. His breath steaming white against the darkness, Simon pressed on up the hill towards the house.

A slave greeted him as he reached the door.

'Welcome—be you *Baptae* or heretic?'

Baptae, Simon had learned from Massiva, was the name that the worshippers of Cotys called themselves.

'I come to take part in tonight's Cottyttia, that's true,' Simon said and slew the slave.

Inside the house, lighted by a single oil-lamp, Simon located the door which opened on reeking blackness. He bent and entered it and soon was creeping downwards, down into the bowels of the hill. The walls of the tunnel were slippery with clammy moss and the air was thick and difficult to breathe. The sharp sound of his sword coming from its scabbard was comforting to Simon.

His sandled feet slipped on the moss-covered stones of the passage and, as he drew nearer to his goal, his heart thudded in his rib-cage and his throat was tight for he now had something of the emotion he had felt when confronted by Alexander's insanity.

Now he heard a low chanting, half ecstatic moaning, half triumphant incantation. The sound grew louder, insinuating itself into his ears until he was caught for a moment in the terrible evil ecstasy which the Cottyttian celebrants were feeling. He controlled himself against an urge to flee, the even stronger urge to join them, and continued to advance, the rare steel sword gleaming in his fist. The iron was a comfort, at least, though he still refused to believe that there was any supernatural agency at work.

Almost tangibly the evil swirled about him as he pressed on and here his rational, doubting nature was to his advantage. Without it, he might easily have succumbed.

The chanting swelled into a great roar of evil joy and through it he heard a name being repeated over and over:

'Cotys. Cotys. Cotys. Cotys.'

He was half hypnotised by the sound, stumbled towards a curtain and wrenched it back.

He retreated a pace at what he saw.

The air was thick with incense. Golden light flared from tall black candles on an altar. From the altar rose a pillar and tied to the pillar was Camilla. She had fainted.

But it was not this that sickened him so much as the sight of the things which swarmed about the altar. They were neither men nor women but neuter. Perhaps they had once been men. They were young and good-looking, their hair long and their faces thin, the bones prominent and the eyes flickering with malignant glee. Naked, to one side of the altar, Simon saw an old woman. Her face was that of a woman of sixty, but her body seemed younger. Around it twined great serpents, caressing her. She crooned to them and led the chanting. Young women danced with the neuters, posturing and prancing.

'Cotys. Cotys. Cotys.'

78

The candles spurted seething light and sent shadows leaping around the walls of the caverns. Then a peculiar golden orange brightness appeared at the top of the column to which Camilla was tied and seemed to twine and coil down the pillar.

Other shapes joined the dancing humans. Twisted shapes with great horns on their heads and the faces of beasts, the hooves of goats.

Simon moved forward, his sword held before him in instinctive protection against the evil in the cavern.

'Cease!' A name came to his lips and he shouted it out: 'In the name of Ormuzd—cease!'

A huge swelling of unhuman laughter came from the boiling brightness on the pillar and Simon saw figures form in it. Figures that were man-shaped and seemed to be at the same time part of the structure of a huge face, lined and pouched with a toothless, gaping mouth and closed eyes.

Then the eyes opened and seemed to fix themselves on Simon. The smaller figures writhed about it and it laughed again. Bile was in his throat, his head throbbed, but he gripped the sword and pushed his way through the sweating bodies of the worshippers. They grinned at him maliciously but did not attempt to stop him.

He was lost in the pull of those malicious eyes.

'Ormuzd is too weak to protect thee, mortal,' the mouth said. 'Ahriman rules here—and will soon rule the world through his vessel, Alexander.'

Still Simon pushed his way towards the pillar, towards Camilla and the leering face above her.

'Ormuzd will not aid thee, mortal. We are many and stronger. Behold me! What do you see?'

Simon made no reply. He gripped the steel blade tighter and advanced closer.

'Do you see us all? Do you see the one these revellers call Cotys? Do you see the Evil One?'

Simon staggered forwards, the last few paces between him and the entity coiling about the pillar. Olympias now pushed her face forward, the snakes hissing, their forked tongues flickering.

'Go to her, Thracian—my son knows thee—go to her and we'll have a double sacrifice, this night.'

With his free hand, Simon pushed against the scaly bodies of the snakes and sent the woman staggering back.

With trancelike deliberation he cut the bonds that held Camilla to the pillar. But many hands, orange-gold hands, shot out from the column and gripped him a shuddering, yet ecstatic embrace. He howled and smote at the hands and, at the touch of steel they flickered back again into their scintillating parent body.

Then he felt the clammy hands of the acolytes upon his body. Sensing that he had some advantage, Simon dragged a bunch of herbs from his shirt—herbs which Massiva had given him—and plunged them into the candle flames. A pungent aroma began to come from the flaring herbs and the naked worshippers dropped back. The apparition itself seemed to fade slightly, its light less bright.

Simon sprang at the shape, his sword flashing like silver and passing through the hazy face which snarled and laughed alternately. The sword clanged on the stone of the column. Desperately, he drew back his arm to strike another blow, his whole body weakened. He felt like an old, worn man.

'Ormuzd!' he shouted as he struck again.

Again the face snarled at him; again the golden hands shot out to embrace him so that his body thrilled with terrible weakening joy.

Then Simon felt that he were all his ancestors and a knowledge came to him, the knowledge of darkness and chaos which his forebears had possessed.

And this knowledge, though terrifying, contained within it a further knowledge—the awareness that the Forces of Darkness had been vanquished in the past and could be vanquished again.

This gave him strength. Ahriman-Cotys realised that from somewhere Simon had gained renewed energy and its shape drew in on itself, began to slide down the pillar towards Camilla.

But Simon reached her, tugged her away from the column and on to the ground. Then he drew back his arm and flung the flaming herbs into the face of the apparition.

A horrid growling sound filled the air, and, for a moment,

the face faded entirely.

Simon grasped Camilla and fell back through the crowd, slashing at their naked bodies with his bright sword. Blood flowed and face reappeared, bellowing with laughter.

Many little faces joined in the merriment, piping their mirth and detaching themselves from the greater entity to fall upon the blood of the slain.

Simon observed, with a degree of relief, that the beings could not pass through the smoke from the herbs and, by this time, the whole room was full of the pungent odour.

'Nothing can destroy us, mortal!' Ahriman-Cotys bellowed. 'Slay more—give me more! You may escape now—but I will sport with you both soon. The huntsmen of my servitor, Olympias, will hound you across the earth. You cannot escape. And when you are ours—you will both become the most willing of my slaves...'

Simon reached the doorway of the cavern, turned, bearing the insensible Camilla and ran up the slippery tunnel.

Now he knew. Now he could not longer rationalise. He had seen too much.

Now he knew that reason had passed from the world and that the ancient gods had returned to rule once more.

CHAPTER FIVE

The body was strong enough. Ahriman had tested it to his satisfaction. He had given the vessel superhuman strength and vitality which it had used for what it thought were its own purposes.

Alexander, though he possessed little of his own personality now, was ready. Soon entire populations would be the slaves of Ahriman, their bodies bent to him. Darkness such as the world had never known would come. Ormuzd and the Forces of Light would be vanquished for ever.

Ahriman had many facets—many names. Shaitan was another.

Now Alexander's captains gathered. They were loyal to him,

would do his bidding—would become Ahriman's agents in bringing Hell to the surface of the Earth.

323 B.C. A time of omens of evil. A turning point in history.

Alexander rose from his bed. He walked like an automaton and called for his slaves. They washed him, dressed him, and clad him in his golden armour.

'Hail, Jupiter-Ammon!' they intoned as he strode from the room and walked steadily to the chamber where his generals and advisors awaited him.

Ptolemy stood up as Alexander entered. His master seemed no different, yet there was a strange, detached air about him.

'Greetings, Jupiter-Ammon,' he said bowing low. Normally he refused to designate Alexander by the name of the God— but this time he was wary, remembering perhaps how Alexander had killed his close friend Clitus in Bactria.

Anaxarchus also bowed. The remaining ten did the same.

Alexander seated himself in the middle of the long table. The leather joints of the golden armour groaned as he bent. There was food and maps on the table. He stuffed a bit of bread into his mouth and unrolled a map, chewing. The twelve men waited nervously for him to speak.

Studying the map, Alexander held out his goblet. Ptolemy filled it with wine from a long-necked bottle of brass. Alexander drank it in a single gulp. Ptolemy replenished the cup.

Simon and Camilla had fled from Pela. The night was like a clammy cloak about them and lightning split the sky, rain hurling itself like tiny spears against their faces.

Camilla rode slightly behind Simon, following him in a terror-filled flight towards the East.

There was no other direction they might go and Simon needed to find Abaris the Magi and get his help, though Alexander still dwelled in Babylon.

Behind them now they heard the Huntsmen of Olympias— great dogs baying, horns sounding, and wild shouts urging the hounds on. And these huntsmen were not mortal—but loaned to Olympias by Ahriman that they both might sport with the fleeing humans.

They caught glimpses of their pursuers—things of legend. Offspring of Cerberus, the three-headed dog which guarded the gates of Hades—dogs with the tails of serpents and with snakes twining round their necks, great, flat hideous-eyed heads, and huge teeth.

The huntsmen rode on the progeny of Pegasus, winged horses which skimmed over the ground, white and beautiful, fast as the North Wind.

And on the backs of the horses—the huntsmen. The grinning shades of dead villains, spewed from Hades to do Ahriman's work. Beside them loped the leopard-women, the Maenades, worshippers of Bacchus.

Behind all these came a screaming multitude of ghouls, demons and were-beasts, released from the depths of Hell.

For two weeks they had been thus pursued and Simon and Camilla were well aware that they could have been caught many times. Ahriman—as he had threatened—was sporting with them.

But still they pushed their horses onwards until they had reached the Bosphorus, hired a boat, and were on the open sea.

Then came the new phantoms to haunt them. Sea-shapes, rearing reptilian monsters, things with blazing eyes which swam just beneath the surface and occasionally put clawed hands on the sides of the boat.

Simon realised at least that all this was calculated to torment them and drive them mad, to give in to Ahriman's evil will.

Camilla, Simon could see, was already beginning to weaken. But he kept tight hold of sanity—and his purpose. Whether the Fates wished it or not, he knew what he must do, had taken upon himself a mission. He refused to attend to anything but that—and his strength aided Camilla.

Soon, Simon knew, the Evil One would realise that he could not break his spirit—then they would be doomed for Ahriman had the power to snuff them out. He prayed to Ormuzd, in whom he now believed with a fervency stemming from his deep need of something to which he could cling, and prayed that he might have a little more time—time to get to Babylon and do what he had taken upon himself to do.

Over the barren plains of Asia Minor they rode and all the nights of their journey the wild huntsmen screamed in their wake until Simon at least could turn sometimes and laugh at

83

them, taunting them with words which were half-mad ravings.

He had little time, he knew.

One night, while great clouds loomed across the sky, they lost their way.

Simon had planned to follow the Euphrates, on the banks of which was built Babylon, but in the confusion of the shrieking night he lost his way and it was not until the following morning that they sighted a river.

With relief, they rode towards it. The days were theirs—no phantoms came to torment them in the sunlight. Soon, Simon felt with a feeling of elation, they would be in Babylon with Abaris and the Magi to aid them against the hordes of Ahriman.

All day they rode, keeping to the cracked bed of the river, dried in the heat of the searing sun. When dusk came, Simon calculated, they should reach the outskirts of Babylon. Which was well, for their horses were by now gaunt skeletons, plodding and tripping in the river bed, and Camilla was swaying, pale and fainting, in the saddle.

The sun began to go down lividly on the horizon as they urged the weary horses forward and already in their ears they heard the faint howling of the Maenades, the insane howlings of Cerburus's spawn. The nightmare of the nights was soon to begin again.

'Pray to Ormuzd that we reach the city in time,' Simon said wearily.

'Another such night and I fear my sanity will give way,' Camilla replied.

The howling, insensate cries of the Bacchae grew louder in their ears and, turning in the saddle, Simon saw behind him the dim shapes of their pursuers—shapes which grew stronger with the deepening darkness.

They turned the bend in the river and the shape of a city loomed ahead.

But then, as they drew closer, Simon's heart fell.

This desolate, jagged ruin, this vast and deserted place was not Babylon! This city was dead—a place where a man, also, might die.

Now the armies of Alexander gathered. And they gathered,

84

unbeknownst to them, not for material conquest but for a greater conquest—to destroy the powers of Light and ensure the powers of Darkness of lasting rule.

Great armies gathered, all metal and leather and disciplined flesh.

323 B.C. and a sick man, drawing vitality from a supernatural source—a man possessed—ruled the known world, ordered its fighting men, controlled its inhabitants.

Alexander of Macedonia. Alexander the Great. Son of Zeus, Jupiter-Ammon. He had united the world under a single monarch—himself. And, united, it would fall . . .

In Babylon, oldest city of the ancient world, Alexander gave his orders to his captains. One hundred and forty-four miles square was Babylon, flanking each side of the great River Euphrates, embanked with walls of brick, closed by gates of bronze. Dominating the city was the Temple of Baal, rising upwards and consisting of eight storeys gradually diminishing in width, ascended by a flight of steps winding around the whole building on the outside. Standing on its topmost tower, Alexander surveyed the mighty city which he had chosen as the base for his military operations. From here he could see the fabulous hanging gardens built by Nebuchadnezzar, laid out upon terraces which were raised one above the other on arches. The streets of the city were straight, intersecting one another at right angles.

Babylon which had brooded for centuries, producing scientists, scholars, artists, great kings, and great priests, splendid warriors, and powerful conquerors. Babylon, whose rulers, the Chaldaeans, worshipped the heavenly bodies and let them guide their law-making.

Babylon, city of secrets and enlightenment. Babylon, soon to be abased by the most terrible blight of evil the world had known. The forces of light were scattered, broken by Alexander's conquerings and Alexander himself had become the focus for the forces of evil. Soon the world would sink into darkness.

Desperately the adherents of Light strove to find a way to stop him, but they were weakened, outlawed. Little pockets of them, chief of these being the Magi of Persia, strove to stand against him—but it was almost futile. Slowly, surely, implacably, evil Ahriman and his minions were gaining ascendancy.

And Simon of Byzantium had failed to reach Babylon and contact the Magi.

Simon and Camilla had never seen such a vast city. The crumbling walls encompassed a fantastic area ... Where they were still intact three chariots might have passed each other on them and they were over 100 feet high. Broken towers rose everywhere, hundreds of them, twice as high as the walls.

But the wind moaned in the towers and great owls with wide, terrible eyes hooted and glided about them, seeming the city's only occupants.

Camilla reached over and found Simon's hand. He gripped it to give her a comfort he did not himself feel.

Behind them they still heard the hunters. Wearied, they could go no further and their tired brains told them that here, among ruins, they would find no hiding place.

The slow clopping of their horses' hooves echoed in the empty city as they followed a broad, overgrown avenue through jagged shadows thrown by the broken buildings. Now Simon could see that the city had been destroyed by fire. But it was cold, chillingly cold in the light of the huge moon which hung overhead like an omen of despair.

The cries of the huntsmen joined the hoots of the owls, a horrid cacophony of fearful, foreboding sound.

But now they could no longer run before their hunters. Fatalistically they must wait—to be caught.

Then suddenly, ahead of them, Simon saw a dark shape framed against the moonlight. He drew his sword and halted his horse. He was too tired to attack, waited for the figure to approach.

When it came closer it flung back the cowl of its cloak and Simon gasped in relief and astonishment.

'Abaris! I was going to seek you in Babylon. What are you doing here?'

'Waiting for you, Simon.' The priest smiled gently and sympathetically. He, also, looked dreadfully worn. His long un-Persian face was pale and there were lines about his mouth.

'Waiting for me? How could you have known that I should lose my way and come here?'

'It was ordained by the Fates that you should do so. Do not

question that.'

'Where are we?'

'In the ruins of forgotten Nineveh. This was a great city once, larger than Babylon and almost as powerful. The Medes and Babylonians razed it 300 years ago.'

'Nineveh,' Camilla breathed, 'there are legends about it.'

'Forget those you have heard and remember this—you are safe here, but not for long. The remnants of Ormuzd's supporters fled here and form a strong company—but not so strong that we can last forever against Ahriman's dreadful minions.'

'Now I realise what happened,' Simon said. 'We followed the Tigris rivers instead of the Euphrates.'

'That is so.'

Behind them the wild baying came closer. Abaris signed to them to follow him.

Abaris led them into a dark sidestreet and then into a maze of alleys choked with fallen masonry, weed-grown and dank. By a small two-storied house which was still virtually intact, he stopped, withdrew a bolt and motioned them inside. They took their horses with them.

The house was much larger inside than it seemed and Simon guessed that it consisted of several houses now. There were about two hundred people in the large room behind the one they had entered. They sat, squatted, and stood in positions of acute weariness. Many were priests. Simon recognised several cults.

Here were Chaldaeans, the ruling caste of Babylon, proud and arrogant seeming still, Egyptian priests of Osiris, a Hebrew rabbi. Others Simon did not recognise and Abaris whispered answers to his questions. There were Brahmin from India, Pythagoreans from Samos and Crotona in Etrusca, Parsees from the deserts of Kerman and Hindustan, Druids from the far North, from the bleak islands on the world's edge, blind priests of the Cimmerians who, history told, were the ancestors of the Thracians and Macedonians.

Alexander had destroyed their temples, scattered them. Only in the far North and the far East were the priests of Light still organised and they had sent deputations to Nineveh to aid their brothers.

And Alexander's wrath had been mainly turned on the Zoroastrians, the Persian and Chaldaean Magi, strongest of the sects who worshipped the powers of Law and Light.

Here they all were, weary men, tired by a battle which required no material weapons yet sapped their vitality as they strove to hold Ahriman at bay.

Abaris introduced Simon and Camilla to the gathering, and he appeared to know the best part of their story, how they had been present at the Cottyttia, how they had fled from Pela, hounded by the infernal hordes, crossed the Bosphorus and came, at length, to fallen Nineveh.

Outside, Nineveh's streets were filled with a hideous throng, weird beasts of all kinds, dead souls, and malevolent denizens of Hell. Three-headed, snake-tailed dogs, winged horses, chimerae, basilisks, sphinx, centaurs and griffins, fire-spewing salamanders. All roamed the broken streets hunting for Ahriman's prey. But there was an area where they could not pass—an area which gave out emanations which meant death for them, so they avoided this area.

For the meantime, Simon and Camilla were safe. But it was stalemate, for while they were in Nineveh, secure against the forces of evil, Alexander strode the golden towers of Babylon and readied the world for the final conquest.

CHAPTER SIX

Abaris told Simon: 'Alexander slew your friend Hano, the Phoenician a week ago.'

Simon cursed: 'May the Harpies pluck his eyes from his skull!'

Camilla said: 'Do not evoke the Harpies, also. We have enough to contend with.'

Abaris half smiled, waved his hand towards a small table in a corner of the room. 'You had better eat now. You must be very tired.'

Gratefully the pair began to eat, drinking the spiced wine of the Magi—a wine which was unnaturally invigorating. Abaris said, while they ate:

'Ahriman dwells constantly, now, in Alexander's body. He intends to make a final campaign, North and East, to subdue the barbarian tribes of Gaul and the Dark Island, crush the Indian kings, and rule the entire world. And, it seems, he will be able to do all this through his vessel, Alexander—for the whole world already responds to Alexander's whims; he commands the fighting men and a host of subject kings and princes. It will be an easy matter . . .'

'But he must be stopped,' Simon said. 'Have you no means of stopping him?'

'For months we have tried to fight the forces of evil, without success. We have almost given up and wait for the coming of Darkness.'

'I believe I know what can be done,' Simon said, 'and it will be a cleaner method than that used by any of you. With your aid I must get to Babylon—and with your aid I will do what I must.'

'Very well, my friend,' Abaris said, 'tell me what you need.'

Kettle-drums beat and brazen trumpets sounded. The dust swelled into the heated air before the feet of Alexander's armies. Coarse soldiers' voices bellowed orders and the captains rode in military pomp at the head of their armies. Plumes of dyed horse-hair bobbed bright beneath the sun, horses stamped, bedecked in trappings of blue and red and yellow, bronze armour glinted like gold and shields clashed against javelins, lances rose like wheat above the heads of the marching men, their tips bright and shining.

Hard-faced warriors moved in ordered ranks—men from Macedonia, Thrace, Greece, Bactria, Babylon, Persia, Assyria, Arabia, Egypt, and the Hebrew nations.

Millions of fighting men. Millions of souls trained for slaying and destruction.

And ordering them, one man—Alexander the Great. Alexander in his hawk-like helm of gold, standing on the steps of the Temple of Baal in Babylon and readying his hosts for the final conquest. Alexander in the trappings of a Persian monarch, absolute ruler of the civilised world. In his right hand a gleaming sword, in his left the sceptre of the law-giver. In his body, possessing it, flowing through it, dominating it—black evil. Ahriman, Master of Darkness, soon to commit the absolute crime—the destruction of Law, the birth of the Dark Millenium.

Around Babylon, mighty armies were camped and it was easy for Simon to enter the city, for many mercenaries had flocked to fight beneath Alexander's banner.

Wrapped around the Thracian was what seemed to be a simple stained black soldier's cloak, but inside, lining it, was richer stuff marked with curious symbols, the Cloak of the Magi, it served to ward off evil and kept Simon, for the time being, safe from Ahriman's attentions.

That day he stood in the square surrounding the Temple of Baal and heard Ahriman speak through Alexander. It was dangerous for him to do this, he knew, but he had to see the man again.

Alexander addressed the populace.

'People of Babylon, my warriors, the morrow sees the start of our final conquests. Soon no spot of soil, no drop of ocean shall be independent of our Empire. I, Jupiter-Ammon, have come to Earth to cleanse it of heretics, to destroy unbelievers and bring the new age to the world. Those who murmur against me shall die. Those who oppose me shall suffer torments and will wish to die. Those who would halt my plans—they shall never die but will be sent living to Hades. Now the armies are marshalled. Already we control most of the world, save for a few patches to the North and a few to the East. Within months these, also, will be ours. Worship us, my people, for Zeus has returned from Olympus, born of a woman named Olympias, father of the son, son and father are One. We are Jupiter-Ammon and our will is divine!'

The people screamed their exultation at these words and bowed low before the man-god who stood so proud above them.

Only Simon remained standing, clad in his bagged and dusty cloak, his face thin, and his eyes bright. He stared up at Alexander who saw him almost immediately, opened his mouth to order the unbeliever destroyed, and then closed it again.

For long moments the two men stared into one another's eyes—the one representing total evil, the other representing the forces of Light. In that great, hushed city nothing seemed to stir and the air carried only faint sounds of military preparation from behind the city walls.

There was a peculiar communication between them. Simon felt as if he were looking into the Abyss of Hell and yet sensed something else lurking in the eyes—something cleaner that had long since been subdued and almost erased.

Then he was in motion, running for the steps that wound upwards around the Temple of Baal.

He bounded up the steps, twenty, fifty, a hundred and he had still not reached Alexander who stood like a statue awaiting him.

The God-Emperor turned as Simon finally reached the upper level. As if Simon were not there he strode back through the shaded pillars and into the building. That was where Simon confronted him.

Sunlight lanced through the pillars and criss-crossed the place in a network of shadow and light. Alexander now sat on a huge golden throne, his chin resting in one hand, his back bent as if in meditation. Steps led up to the dais on which the throne was placed. Simon stopped at the first step and looked up at the conqueror of the world.

Alexander leaned back in his throne and clasped his hands in front of him. He smiled slowly, at first a smile of irony which twisted into a grin of malice and hatred.

'There is a sacred bull in Memphis,' Alexander said slowly, 'which is called Apis. It is an oracle. Seven years ago I went to Memphis to hear the sacred bull and to ascertain whether it had, indeed, oracular powers. When it saw me it spoke a rhyme. I have remembered that rhyme for seven years.'

Simon drew the Cloak of the Magi closer about him. 'What did it say?' he asked in a strained half-whisper.

Alexander shook his head. 'I did not understand it until recently. It went——

> *The City that thy father lost shall fall to thee,*
> *The City that gives birth to fools shall bear a sword.*
> *The City that thy father lost shall be its home.*
> *The City that ye make thy home shall feel its edge.'*

Simon brooded over this for a moment and then he nodded, understanding.

'Byzantium, Abdera, Byzantium—Babylon,' he said.

91

'How sharp is the sword?' Alexander asked and changed shape.

A dazzling orange-golden haze burst upwards and a black and scarlet figure stood framed in the centre. It vaguely resembled Alexander but was twice as high, twice as broad, and bore a weirdly wrought staff in its hand.

'So!' Simon cried, 'At last you show your true shape. You bear the Wand of Ahriman, I see!'

'Aye, mortal—and that only Ahriman may bear.'

From beneath the Cloak of the Magi, Simon produced a short javelin and a small shield of about ten inches in diameter. He held the shield in front of his face and through it could see unnerving and alien shapes where the figure of Ahriman stood. He was seeing the true shape of Ahriman, not the warped and metamorphosed body of Alexander.

He drew back his arm and hurled the javelin at a certain spot in the intricate supernatural pattern.

There came an unearthly groaning and muttering from the figure. It threw up its arms and the wand flickered and sent a bolt of black lightning at Simon who put up his shield again and repelled it, though he was hurled back against a far column. He leaped to his feet, drawing his sword and saw that, as Abaris had told him, Alexander had resumed his usual shape.

The God-King staggered and frowned. He turned and saw Simon standing there, sword in hand.

'What's this?' he said.

'Prepare to fight me, Alexander!' Simon cried.

'But why?'

'You must never know why.'

And Simon leaped forward.

Alexander drew his own lovely blade, a slim thing of strong tempering, of glowing star-metal with a handle of black onyx.

The iron clashed with a musical note, so fine were both blades and the two men feinted, parried, and stabbed, fighting in the Greek manner, using the points of their swords rather than the edges.

Alexander came in swiftly, grasped Simon's wrist and pushed his sword back, bringing his own sword in, but Simon sidestepped just in time, and the blade grazed his thigh. Alexander cursed a very human curse and grinned briefly at Simon

92

in the old, earlier manner.

'You are swift, my friend.'

Simon disliked this. It was harder to fight such a light-hearted and likeable warrior than the thing which Alexander had earlier been. It was almost unjust—yet the action had to be made.

In and out of the network of light and shadow the two men danced, skipping away, coming in close, swords flashing, and the music of their meeting echoing about the Temple of Baal.

Then Alexander's soldiers came running into the place but Alexander cried:

'Stand back—I do not know why this man attacked me, but I have never fought such a swordsman before and would not miss the privilege. If he wins—free him.'

Bewildered, the guards retreated.

For hours the fight continued, each man evenly matched. Dusk came, sunset flooding the Temple with blood-red rays. Like two archetypal gods they fought on, thrusting, parrying, employing every tactic at their command.

Then Alexander, whose earlier sickness had wearied him, stumbled and Simon saw his opportunity. Paused, deliberating the act, then rushed upon his opponent and struck him a terrible thrust in the lung.

'Go—be Charon's guest!' he cried.

Alexander went hurtling back to land with a crash, sprawled on the steps to the dais. Again the watching warriors rushed forward, but Alexander waved them back.

'Do not tell the people how I met my end,' he gasped. 'I have united the world—let it stay united in the confidence that a—a—god created that unity. Perhaps that will serve to ensure peace . . .'

Dismissed, the guards returned, wondering, down the steps of the Temple and Simon and the dying Alexander were left alone in the half-light while a wind blew up and sent a cold chill through the silent columns.

'I remember you now,' Alexander said, blood beginning to trickle from his mouth. 'You are the Thracian. What happened—I remember interviewing you and then the rest is hazed in blackness and chaos—what happened then?'

Simon shook his head.

'Call it madness,' he said. 'A madness, which came upon you.'

In the shadows behind the throne he saw a black mist begin to form. Hurriedly he shouted: 'Abaris—quickly!'

The priest appeared then. He had slipped up the steps and had been standing behind a column. Others followed him. He motioned them in. They began a weird and beautiful chanting, advancing towards the hazy form behind the throne, making peculiar passes in the air.

After them, Camilla appeared and stood framed in a gap between two columns, the wind ruffling her hair.

Alexander grasped Simon's arm. 'I remember a prophesy—one made by the Oracle of Memphis. How did it go?'

Simon quoted it.

'Yes,' Alexander gasped. 'So you are the sword which the City of Fools, Abdera, bore...'

'What shall we remember of you, Alexander?' Simon asked quietly as there came a commotion behind the throne which was now surrounded by chanting Magi. He looked up. The priests seemed to be straining to hold back some horrible force which whimpered and moaned at them, yet was still very strong.

'Remember? Will not the world always remember me? My dream was to unite the world and bring peace. But a nightmare interrupted that dream, I think...'

'Your father's dream and yours,' Simon said.

'My father—I hated him—yet he was a good and wise king and moulded me for a purpose. Aristotle was my teacher, you know. But I had other indoctrination. My mother Olympias, taught me peculiar things which I cannot remember now.'

'Let us hope no one shall ever know them again,' Simon breathed.

'What has happened?' Alexander asked again. Then his eyes closed. 'What did I do?'

'You did nothing that was not for the good of the world,' Simon told him. Alexander was dead. 'But,' the Thracian added quietly as the Emperor's grip loosened and the limp hand fell to the marble of the step, 'that which possessed you wrought harm. You could not help it. You were born to perish...'

He rose and called: 'Abaris. Abaris—he is dead.'

The chanting ceased. The black shape still hovered there, veins of orange-gold, black, and scarlet throbbing in it like blood-vessels. Simon and the priests fell back.

The shape shot towards Alexander's corpse, sank down over it. The corpse jerked but then was still again. For an instant a face—the face Simon had seen at the Rites of Cotys in Pela—appeared.

'There will be others, never fear!' Ahriman said and vanished.

Abaris went over to Alexander's corpse and made a pass over the wound. When Simon looked there was no sign of a wound.

'We'll say he died of a fever,' Abaris said softly. 'It was well known that he was ill. They will believe us—we will let the Chaldaeans speak in Babylon for they long ruled the people before Alexander's coming.'

Simon said: 'I knew that clean steel could end this matter for us.'

Abaris looked at him a trifle cynically.

'Without our magic to drive Ahriman out of Alexander's body for the time you needed, you would never have succeeded.'

'That's true, I suppose.'

Abaris continued:

'That was the solution. Ahriman works through many people —but he needs a single human vessel if he is to carry out his Great Plan. Several have been born in the past—others will be born again. Fanatical conquerors who will set out to rule the world. Men with superhuman vitality, the power of dominating great masses of people and driving them to do that one man's will. Yes, Ahriman—under whatever name he takes—will try again. That is certain.'

'Meanwhile,' Simon said as Camilla came up to him, 'we have succeeded in halting Ahriman this time.'

'Who knows?' Abaris said. 'History will show if we were in time or not.'

Simon said gravely: 'I am not sure what Alexander, himself, was. He could have been a force for good or evil. He was something of both. But the evil gained ascendancy towards the end. Was I right to kill him? Could not his course have been turned so that the good in him could have continued his plan to unite the world in peace?'

'That may have been possible,' the priest said thoughtfully, 'but we men set limits to our endeavours—it is easier that way. Perhaps, in time, we will not stop short but will learn to choose the harder paths and so achieve more positive results. As it is we strive merely to keep a balance. One day Alexander's dream may be realised and the world united. Let us hope that the unity will be inspired by Ormuzd. Then it may be possible to build.'

Simon sighed and made his body relax.

TO RESCUE TANELORN...

CHAPTER ONE

Beyond the tall and ominous glass-green forest of Troos, well to the North and unheard of in Bakshaan, Elwher or any other city of the Young Kingdoms, on the shifting shores of the Sighing Desert lay Tanelorn, a lonely, long-ago city, loved by those it sheltered.

Tanelorn had a peculiar nature in that it welcomed and held the wanderer. To its peaceful streets and low houses came the gaunt, the savage, the brutalised, the tormented, and in Tanelorn they found rest.

Now, most of these troubled travellers who dwelt in peaceful Tanelorn had thrown off earlier allegiances to the Lords of Chaos who, as gods, took more than a mild interest in the affairs of men. It happened, therefore, that these same Lords grew to resent the unlikely city of Tanelorn and, at length, decided to act.

They instructed one of their number (more they could not send) Lord Narjhan, to journey to Nadsokor, the City of Beggars, and raise an army that would attack undefended Tanelorn and destroy it and its inhabitants. So he did this, arming his ragged army and promising them many things.

Then, like a ferocious tide, did the beggar rabble set off to tear down Tanelorn and slay its residents. A great torrent of men and women in rags, on crutches, blind, maimed, but moving steadily, ominously, implacably Northwards towards the Sighing Desert.

In Tanelorn dwelt the Red Archer, Rackhir, from the Eastlands beyond the Sighing Desert, beyond the Weeping Waste. Rackhir had been born a Warrior Priest, a servant of the Lords of Chaos, but had forsaken this life for the quieter pursuits of thievery and learning. A man with harsh features slashed from the bone of his skull, strong, fleshless nose, deep eye-cavities, a thin mouth and a thin beard. He wore a red skull-cap, decorated

97

with a hawk's feather, a red jerkin, tight-fitting and belted at the waist, red breeks, and red boots. It was as if all the blood in him had transferred itself to his gear and left him drained. He was happy, however, in Tanelorn, the city which made all such men happy, and felt he would die there if men died there. He did not know if they did.

One day he saw Brut of Lashmar, a great, blond-headed noble of shamed name, ride wearily, yet urgently, through the low wall-gate of the city of peace. Brut's silver harness and trappings were begrimed, his yellow cloak torn and his broad-brimmed hat battered. A small crowd collected around him as he rode into the city square and halted. Then he gave his news.

'Beggars from Nadsokor, many thousands, move against our Tanelorn,' he said, 'and they are led by Narjhan of Chaos.'

Now, all the men in there were soldiers of some kind, good ones for the most part, and they were confident warriors, but few in number. A horde of beggars, led by such a being as Narjhan, could destroy Tanelorn, they knew.

'Should we, then, leave Tanelorn?' said Uroch of Nieva, a young, wasted man who had been a drunkard.

'We owe this city too much to desert her,' Rackhir said. 'We should defend her—for her sake and ours. There will never be such a city again.'

Brut leaned forward in his saddle and said: 'In principle, Red Archer, I am in agreement with you. But principle is not enough without deeds. How would you suggest we defend this low-walled city against siege and the powers of Chaos?'

'We should need help,' Rackhir replied, 'supernatural help if need be.'

'Would the Grey Lords help us?' Zas the One-handed asked the question. He was an old, torn wanderer who had once gained a throne and lost it again.

'Aye—the Grey Lords!' Several voices chorused this hopefully.

'Who are the Grey Lords?' said Uroch, but no one heard him.

'They are not inclined to aid anyone at all,' Zas the One-handed pointed out, 'but surely a neutral city such as Tanelorn, coming as it does under neither the Forces of Law nor the Lords of Chaos, would be worth their while preserving. After all, they have no loyalties either.'

'I'm for seeking the Grey Lords' aid,' Brut nodded. 'What of the rest of us?' There was general agreement, then silence when they realised that they knew of no means of contacting the mysterious and insouciant beings. At last Zas pointed this out.

Rackhir said: 'I know a seer—a hermit who lives in the Sighing Desert. Perhaps he can help?'

'I think that, after all, we should not waste time looking for supernatural assistance against this beggar rabble,' Uroch said. 'Let us prepare, instead, to meet the attack with physical means.'

'You forget,' Brut said wearily, 'that they are led by Narjhan of Chaos. He is not human and has the whole strength of Chaos behind him. We know that the Grey Lords are pledged neither to Law nor to Chaos but will sometimes help either side if the whim takes them. They are our only chance.'

'Why not seek the aid of the Forces of Law, sworn enemies of Chaos and mightier than the Grey Lords?' Uroch said.

'Because Tanelorn is a neutral city owing alliegance to neither side. We are all of us men and women who have broken our pledge to Chaos but have made no new one to Law. The Forces of Law are just but, in matters of this kind, will help only those sworn to them. We are renegades—the Grey Lords only may protect us, if they would.' So said Zas.

'I will go to find my seer,' Rackhir the Red Archer said, 'and if he knows how I may reach the Domain of the Grey Lords, then I'll continue straight on, for there is so little time. If I reach them and solicit their help you will soon know I have done so. If not, you must die in Tanelorn's defence and, if I live, I will join you in that last battle.'

'Very well,' Brut agreed, 'go quickly, Red Archer. Let one of your own arrows be the measure of your speed.'

And taking little with him save his bone bow and quiver of scarlet-fletched arrows, Rackhir set off for the Sighing Desert.

From Nadsokor, South West through the land of Vilmir, even through the squalid country of Org which has in it the dreadful forest of Troos, there was flame and black horror in the wake of the beggar horde, and insolent, disdainful of them though he led them, rode a being completely clad in black armour with a voice that rang hollow in the helm. People fled away at their approach and the lands of Vilmir, Org, and Ilmiora were made barren by their passing. Most knew what had happened, that the beggar citizens of Nadsokor had, contrary to their traditions of centuries, vomited from their city in a wild, menacing horde. Someone had armed them—someone had made them go Northwards and Westwards towards the Sighing Desert. But who was the one who led them? Ordinary folk did not know. And why did they head for the Sighing Desert? There was no city beyond Karlaak, which they had skirted, only the Sighing Desert—and beyond that the edge of the world. Was that their destination? Were they heading, lemming-like, to their destruction? Everyone hoped so, in their hate for the horrible horde.

Rackhir rode through the mournful wind of the Sighing Desert, his face and eyes protected against the particles of sand which flew about. He was thirsty and had been riding a day. Ahead of him at last were the rocks he sought.

He reached the rocks and called above the wind.

'Lamsar!'

The hermit came out in answer to Rackhir's shout. He was dressed in oiled leather to which sand clung. His beard, too, was encrusted with sand and his skin seemed to have taken on the colour and texture of the desert. He recognised Rackhir immediately, by his dress, beckoned him into the cave, and disappeared back inside. Rackhir dismounted and led his horse to the cave entrance and went in.

Lamsar was seated on a smooth rock. 'You are welcome, Red Archer,' he said, 'and I perceive by your manner that you wish information from me and that your mission is urgent.'

'I seek the help of the Grey Lords, Lamsar,' said Rackhir.

The old hermit smiled. It was as if a fissure had suddenly appeared in a rock. 'To risk the journey through the Five Gates, your mission must be important. I will tell you how to reach the Grey Lords, but the road is a difficult one.'

'I'm willing to take it,' Rackhir replied, 'for Tanelorn is threatened and the Grey Lords could help her.'

'Then you must pass through the First Gate, which lies in

100

our own dimension. I will help you find it.'

'And what must I do then?'

'You must pass through all five gates. Each gateway leads to a world which lies beyond and within our own dimension. On each world you must speak with the dwellers there. Some are friendly to men, some are not, but all must answer your question: 'Where lies the next Gate?' though some may seek to stop you passing. The last gate leads to the Grey Lords' Domain.'

'And the first gate?'

'That lies anywhere on Earth. I will find it for you now.'

Lamsar composed himself to meditate and Rackhir, who had expected some sort of gaudy miracle-working from the old man, was disappointed.

Several hours went by until Lamsar said: 'The gate is outside. Memorise the following: If X is equal to the spirit of humanity, then the combination of the two must be of double power, therefore the spirit of humanity always contains the power to dominate itself.'

'A strange equation,' said Rackhir.

'Aye—but memorise it, meditate upon it and then we will leave.'

'We—you as well?'

'I think so.'

Rackhir liked Lamsar, but the hermit was old. He did not want him on the journey. But then he realised that the hermit's knowledge could be of use to him, so did not object. He thought upon the equation and, as he thought, his mind seemed to glitter and become diffused until he was in a strange trance and all his powers felt greater, both those of mind and body. The hermit got up and Rackhir followed him. They went out of the cave-mouth but, instead of the Sighing Desert, there was a hazy cloud of blue shimmering light ahead and when they had passed through this, in a second, they found themselves in the foothills of a low mountain-range and below them, in a valley, were villages. The villages were strangely laid out, all the houses in a wide circle about a huge amphitheatre containing, at its centre, a circular dais.

'It will be interesting to learn the reason why these villages are so laid out,' Lamsar said, and they began to move down into the valley.

As they reached the bottom and came close to one of the villages, people came gaily out and danced joyfully towards them. They stopped in front of Rackhir and Lamsar and, jumping from foot to foot as he greeted them, the leader spoke.

'You are strangers, we can tell—and you are welcome to all we have, food, accommodation, and entertainment.'

The two men thanked them graciously and accompanied them back to the circular village. The amphitheatre was made of mud and seemed to have been stamped out, hollowed into, the ground encompassed by the houses. The leader of the villagers took them to his house and offered them food.

'You have come to us at a Rest Time,' he said, 'but do not worry, things will soon commence again. My name is Yerleroo.'

'We seek the next Gate,' Lamsar said politely, 'and our mission is urgent. You will forgive us if we do not stay long?'

'Come,' said Yerleroo, 'things are about to commence. You will see us at our best, and must join us.'

All the villagers had assembled in the amphitheatre, surrounding the platform in the centre. Most of them were light-skinned and light-haired, gay and smiling, excited—but a few were evidently of a different race, dark, black-haired, and these were sullen.

Sensing something ominous in what he saw, Rackhir asked the question directly: 'Where is the next Gate?'

Yerleroo hesitated, his mouth worked and then he smiled. 'Where the winds meet,' he said.

Rackhir declared angrily: 'That's no answer.'

'Yes it is,' said Lamsar softly behind him. 'A fair answer.'

'Now we shall dance,' Yerleroo said. 'First you shall watch our dance and then you shall join in.'

'Dance?' said Rackhir, wishing he had brought a sword, or at least a dagger.

'Yes—you will like it. Everyone likes it. You will find it will do you good.'

'What if we do not wish to dance?'

'You must—it is for your own good, be assured.'

'And he——' Rackhir pointed at one of the sullen men. 'Does he enjoy it?'

'It is for his own good.'

102

Yerleroo clapped his hands and at once the fair-haired people leapt into a frenetic, senseless dance. Some of them sang. The sullen people did not sing. After a little hesitation, they began to prance dully about, their frowning features contrasting with their jerking bodies. Soon the whole village was dancing, whirling, singing a monotonous song.

Yerleroo flashed by, whirling. 'Come, join in now.'

'We had better leave,' Lamsar said with a faint smile. They backed away.

Yerleroo saw them. 'No—you must not leave—you must dance.'

They turned and ran as fast as the old man could go. The dancing villagers changed the direction of their dance and began to whirl menacingly towards them in a horrible semblance of gaiety.

'There's nothing for it,' Lamsar said and stood his ground, observing them through ironic eyes. 'The mountain gods must be invoked. A pity, for sorcery wearies me. Let us hope their magic extends to this plane. *Gordar!*'

Words in an unusually harsh language issued from Lamsar's old mouth. The whirling villagers came on.

Lamsar pointed at them.

The villagers became suddenly petrified and slowly, disturbingly, their bodies caught in a hundred positions, turned to smooth, black basalt.

'It was for their own good,' Lamsar smiled grimly. 'Come, to the place where the winds meet,' and he took Rackhir there quite swiftly.

At the place where the winds met they found the second gateway, a column of amber-coloured flame, shot through with streaks of green. They entered it and, instantly, were in a world of dark, seething colour. Above them was a sky of murky red in which other colours shifted, agitated, changing. Ahead of them lay a forest, dark, blue, black, heavy, mottled green, the tops of its trees moving like a wild tide. It was a howling land of unnatural phenomena.

Lamsar pursed his lips. 'On this plane Chaos rules, we must get to the next gate swiftly for obviously the Lords of Chaos will seek to stop us.'

'Is it always like this?' Rackhir gasped.

'It is always boiling midnight—but the rest, it changes with the moods of the Lords. There are no rules at all.'

They pressed on through the bounding, blossoming scenery as it erupted and changed around them. Once they saw a huge winged figure in the sky, smoky yellow, and roughly man-shaped.

'Vezhan,' Lamsar said, 'let's hope he did not see us.'

'Vezhan!' Rackhir whispered the name—for it was to Vezhan that he had once been loyal.

They crept on, uncertain of their direction or even of their speed in that disturbing land.

Chapter Two

At length, they came to the shores of a peculiar ocean.

It was a grey, heaving, timeless sea, a mysterious sea which stretched into infinity. There could be no other shores beyond this rolling plain of water. No other lands or rivers or dark, cool woods, no other men or women or ships. It was a sea which led to nowhere. It was complete to itself—a sea.

Over this timeless ocean hovered a brooding ochre sun which cast moody shadows of black and green across the water, giving the whole scene something of the look of being enclosed in a vast cavern, for the sky above was gnarled and black with ancient clouds. And all the while the doom-carried crash of breakers, the lonely, fated monotony of the ever-rearing white-topped waves; the sound which portended neither death nor life nor war nor peace—simply existence and shifting inharmony. They could go no further.

'This has the air of our death about it,' Rackhir said shivering.

The sea roared and tumbled, the sound of it increasing to a fury, daring them to go on towards it, welcoming them with wild temptation—offering them nothing but achievement—the achievement of death.

Lamsar said: 'It is not my fate to wholly perish.' But then they were running back towards the forest, feeling that the strange sea was pouring up the beach towards them. They looked back and saw that it had gone no further, that the breakers were less wild, the sea more calm. Lamsar was little way behind Rackhir.

The Red Archer gripped his hand and hauled him towards him as if he had rescued the old man from a whirlpool. They remained there, mesmerised, for a long time, while the sea called to them and the wind was a cold caress on their flesh.

In the bleak brightness of the alien shore, under a sun which gave no heat, their bodies shone like stars in the night and they turned towards the forest, quietly.

'Are we trapped, then, in this world of Chaos?' Rackhir said at length. 'If we meet someone, they will offer us harm—how can we ask our question?'

Then there emerged from the huge forest a great figure, naked and gnarled like the trunk of a tree, green as lime, but the face was jovial.

'Greetings, unhappy renegades,' it said.

'Where is the next gate?' said Lamsar quickly.

'You almost entered it, but turned away,' laughed the giant. 'That sea does not exist—it is there to stop travellers from passing through the gate.'

'It exists here, in the world of Chaos,' Rackhir said thickly.

'You could say so—but what exists in Chaos save the disorders of the minds of gods gone mad?'

Rackhir had strung his bone bow and fitted an arrow to the string, but he did it in the knowledge of his own hopelessness.

'Do not shoot the arrow,' said Lamsar softly. 'Not yet.' And he stared at the arrow and muttered.

The giant advanced carelessly towards them, unhurried.

'It will please me to exact the price of your crimes from you,' it said, 'for I am Hionhurn the Executioner. You will find your death pleasant—but your fate unbearable.' And he came closer, his clawed hands outstretched.

'Shoot!' croaked Lamsar and Rackhir brought the bow-string to his cheek, pulled it back with might and released the arrow at the giant's heart. 'Run!' cried Lamsar, and in spite of their forebodings they ran back down the shore towards the frightful sea. They heard the giant groan behind them as they reached the edge of the sea and, instead of running into water, found themselves in a range of stark mountains.

'No mortal arrow could have delayed him,' Rackhir said. 'How did you stop him?'

'I used an old charm—the Charm of Justice, which, when applied to any weapon, makes it strike at the unjust.'

'But why did it hurt Hionhurn, an immortal?' Rackhir asked.

'There is no justice in the world of Chaos—something constant and inflexible, whatever its nature, must harm any servant of the Lords of Chaos.'

'We have passed through the third gate,' Rackhir said, unstringing his bow, 'and have the fourth and fifth to find. Two dangers have been avoided—but what new ones will we encounter now?'

'Who knows?' said Lamsar, and they walked on through the rocky mountain pass and entered a forest that was cool, even though the sun had reached its zenith and was glaring down through parts of the thick foliage. There was an air of ancient calm about the place. They heard unfamiliar bird-calls and saw tiny golden birds which were also new to them.

'There is something calm and peaceful about this place—I almost distrust it,' Rackhir said, but Lamsar pointed ahead silently.

Rackhir saw a large domed building, magnificent in marble and blue mosaic. It stood in a clearing of yellow grass and the marble caught the sun, flashing like fire.

They neared the domed construction and saw that it was supported by big marble columns set into a platform of milky jade. In the centre of the platform, a stairway of blue-stone curved upwards and disappeared into a circular aperture. There were wide windows set into the sides of the raised building but they could not see inside. There were no inhabitants visible and it would have seemed strange to the pair if there had been. They crossed the yellow glade and stepped on to the jade platform. It was warm, as if it had been exposed to the sun. They almost slipped on the smooth stone.

They reached the blue steps and mounted them, staring upwards, but they could still see nothing. They did not attempt to ask themselves why they were so assuredly invading the building; it seemed quite natural that they should do what they were doing. There was no alternative. There was an air of familiarity about the place. Rackhir felt it but did not know why. Inside was a cool, shadowy hall, a blend of soft darkness and bright sunlight which entered by the windows. The floor was pearl-pink and the ceiling deep scarlet. The hall reminded Rackhir of a womb.

Partially hidden by deep shadow was a small doorway and beyond it, steps. Rackhir looked questioningly at Lamsar. 'Do we proceed in our exploration?'

'We must—to have our question answered, if possible.'

They climbed the steps and found themselves in a smaller hall similar to the one beneath them. This hall, however, was furnished with twelve wide thrones placed in a semicircle in the centre. Against the wall, near the door, were several chairs, upholstered in purple fabric. The thrones were of gold, decorated with fine silver, padded with white cloth.

A door behind the throne opened and a tall, fragile-looking man appeared, followed by others whose faces were almost identical. Only their robes were noticeably different. Their faces were pale, almost white, their noses straight, their lips thin but not cruel. Their eyes were unhuman—green-flecked eyes which stared outwards with sad composure. The leader of the tall men looked at Rackhir and Lamsar. He nodded and waved a pale, long-fingered hand gracefully.

'Welcome,' he said. His voice was high and frail, like a girl's, but beautiful in its modulation. The other eleven men seated themselves in the thrones but the first man, who had spoken, remained standing. 'Sit down, please,' he said.

Rackhir and Lamsar sat down on two of the purple chairs.

'How did you come here?' enquired the man.

'Through the gates from Chaos,' Lamsar replied.

'And were you seeking our world?'

'No—we travel towards the Domain of the Grey Lords.'

'I thought so, for your people rarely visit us save by accident.'

'Where are we?' asked Rackhir as the man seated himself in the remaining throne.

'In a place beyond time. Once our land was part of the earth you know, but in the dim past it became separated from it. Our bodies, unlike yours, are immortal. We choose this, but we are not bound to our flesh, as you are.'

'I don't understand,' frowned Rackhir. 'What are you saying?'

'I have said what I can in the simplest terms understandable to you. If you do not know what I say then I can explain no further. We are called the Guardians—though we guard nothing. We are warriors, but we fight nothing.'

'What else do you do?' enquired Rackhir.

'We exist. You will want to know where the next gateway lies?'

'Yes.'

'Refresh yourselves here, and then we shall show you the gateway.'

'What is your function?' asked Rackhir.

'To function,' said the man.

'You are unhuman!'

'We are human. *You* spend your lives chasing that which is within you and that which you can find in any other human being—but you will not look for it there—you must follow more glamorous paths—to waste your time in order to discover that you have wasted your time. I am glad that we are no longer like you—but I wish that it were lawful to help you further. This, however, we may not do.'

'Ours is no meaningless quest,' said Lamsar quietly, with respect. 'We go to rescue Tanelorn.'

'Tanelorn?' the man said softly. 'Does Tanelorn still remain?'

'Aye,' said Rackhir, 'and shelters tired men who are grateful for the rest she offers.' Now he realised why the building had been familiar—it had the same quality, but intensified, as Tanelorn.

'Tanelorn was the last of our cities,' said the Guardian. 'Forgive us for judging you—most of the travellers who pass through this plane are searchers, restless, with no real purpose, only excuses, imaginary reasons for journeying on. You must love Tanelorn to brave the dangers of the gateways?'

'We do,' said Rackhir, 'and I am grateful that you built her.'

'We built her for ourselves, but it is good that others have used her well—and she them.'

'Will you help us?' Rackhir said. 'For Tanelorn?'

'We cannot—it is not lawful. Now, refresh yourselves and be welcome.'

The two travellers were given foods, both soft and brittle, sweet and sour, and drink which seemed to enter the pores of their skin as they quaffed it, and then the Guardian said: 'We have caused a road to be made. Follow it and enter the next world. But we warn you, it is the most dangerous of all.'

And they set off down the road that the Guardians had caused to be made and passed through the fourth gateway into a dreadful world—the world of Law.

CHAPTER THREE

Nothing shone in the grey-light sky, nothing moved, nothing marred the grey.

Nothing interrupted the bleak grey plain stretching on all sides of them, forever. There was no horizon. It was a bright, clean wasteland. But there was a sense about the air, a presence of something past, something which had gone but left a faint aura of its passing.

'What dangers could be here?' said Rackhir shuddering, 'here where there is nothing?'

'The danger of the loneliest madness,' Lamsar replied. Their voices were swallowed in the grey expanse.

'When the Earth was very young,' Lamsar continued, his words trailing away across the wilderness, 'things were like this—but there were seas, there were seas. Here there is nothing.'

'You are wrong,' Rackhir said with a faint smile. 'I have thought—here there is Law.'

'That is true—but what is Law without something to decide between? Here is Law—bereft of justice.'

They walked on, all about them an air of something intangible that had once been tangible. On they walked through this barren world of Absolute Law.

Eventually, Rackhir spied something. Something that flickered, faded, appeared again until, as they neared it, they saw that it was a man. His great head was noble, firm, and his body was massively built, but the face was twisted in a tortured frown and he did not see them as they approached him.

They stopped before him and Lamsar coughed to attract his attention. He turned that great head and regarded them abstractedly, the frown clearing at length, to be replaced by a calmer, thoughtful expression.

'Who are you?' asked Rackhir.

The man sighed. 'Not yet,' he said, 'not yet, it seems. More phantoms.'

'Are *we* the phantoms?' smiled Rackhir. 'That seems to be more your own nature.' He watched as the man began slowly to fade again, his form less definite, melting. The body seemed to make a great heave, like a salmon attempting to leap a dam, then it was back again in a more solid form.

'I had thought myself rid of all that was superfluous, save my own obstinate shape,' the man said tiredly, 'but here is something, back again. Is my reason failing—is my logic no longer what it was?'

'Do not fear,' said Rackhir, 'we are material beings.'

'That is *what* I feared. For an eternity I have been stripping away the layers of unreality which obscure the truth. I have almost succeeded in the final act, and now you begin to creep back. My mind is not what it was, I think.'

'Perhaps you worry lest we do not exist?' Lamsar said slowly, with a clever smile.

'You know that is not so—you do not exist, just as I do not exist.' The frown returned, the features twisted, the body began, again, to fade, only to resume, once more, its earlier nature. The man sighed. 'Even to reply to you is betraying myself, but I suppose a little relaxation will serve to rest my powers and equip me for the final effort of will which will bring me to the ultimate truth—the truth of non-being.'

'But non-being involves non-thought, non-will, non-action,' Lamsar said. 'Surely you would not submit yourself to such a fate?'

'There is no such thing as self. I am the only reasoning thing in creation—I am almost pure reason. A little more effort and I shall be what I desire to be—the one truth in this non-existent universe. That requires first ridding myself of anything ex-

110

traneous around me—such as yourselves—and then making the final plunge into the only reality.'

'What is that?'

'The state of absolute nothingness where there is nothing to disturb the order of things because there *is* no order of things.'

'Scarcely a constructive ambition,' Rackhir said.

'Construction is a meaningless word—like all words, like all so-called existence. Everything means nothing—that is the only truth.'

'But what of this world? Barren as it is, it still has light and firm rock. You have not succeeded in reasoning that out of existence,' Lamsar said.

'That will cease when I cease,' the man said slowly, 'just as you will cease to be. Then there can be nothing but nothing and Law will reign unchallenged.'

'But Law cannot reign—it will not exist either, according to your logic.'

'You are wrong—nothingness is the Law. Nothingness is the object of Law. Law is the way to its ultimate state, the state of non-being.'

'Well,' said Lamsar musingly, 'then you had better tell us where we may find the next gate.'

'There is no gate.'

'If there were, where would we find it?' Rackhir said.

'If a gate existed, and it does not, it would have been inside the mountain, close to what was once called the Sea of Peace.'

'And where was that?' Rackhir asked, conscious, now of their terrible predicament. There were no landmarks, no sun, no stars—nothing by which they could determine direction.

'Close to the Mountain of Severity.'

'Which way do you go?' Lamsar enquired of the man.

'Out—beyond—to nowhere.'

'And where, if you succeed in your object, will *we* be consigned?'

'To some other nowhere. I cannot truthfully answer. But since you have never existed in reality, therefore you can go on to no non-reality. Only I am real—and I do not exist.'

'We are getting nowhere,' said Rackhir with a smirk which changed to a frown as he realised his predicament.

'It is only my mind which holds the non-reality at bay,' the man said, 'and I must concentrate or else it will all come flooding back and I shall have to start from the beginning again. In the beginning, there was everything—chaos. I *created* nothing.'

With resignation, Rackhir strung his bow, fitted an arrow to the string and aimed at the frowning man.

'You wish for non-being?' he said.

'I have told you so.' Rackhir's arrow pierced his heart, his body faded, became solid and slumped to the grass as mountains, forests, and rivers appeared around them. It was still a peaceful, well-ordered world and Rackhir and Lamsar, as they strode on in search of the Mountain of Severity, savoured it. There seemed to be no animal life here and they talked, in puzzled terms, about the man they had been forced to kill, until, at length, they reached a great smooth pyramid which seemed, though it was of natural origin, to have been carved into this form. They walked around its base until they discovered an opening.

There could be no doubt that this was the Mountain of Severity, and a calm ocean lay some distance away. They went into the opening and emerged into a delicate landscape. They were now through the last gateway and in the Domain of the Grey Lords.

There were trees like stiffened spider-webs.

Here and there were blue pools, shallow, with shining water and graceful rocks balanced in them and around their shores. Above them and beyond them the light hills swept away towards a pastel yellow horizon which was tinted with red, orange, and blue, deep blue.

They felt overlarge, clumsy, like crude, gross giants treading on the fine, short grass. They felt as if they were destroying the sanctity of the place.

Then they saw a girl come walking towards them.

She stopped as they came closer to her. She was dressed in loose black robes which flowed about her as if in a wind, but there was no wind. Her face was pale and pointed, her black eyes large and enigmatic. At her long throat was a jewel.

'Sorana,' said Rackhir thickly, 'you died.'

'I disappeared,' said she, 'and this is where I came. I was told that you would come to this place and decided that I would meet you.'

112

'But this is the Domain of the Grey Lords—and you serve Chaos.'

'I do—but many are welcome at the Grey Lords' Court, whether they be of Law, Chaos, or neither. Come, I will escort you there.'

Bewildered, now, Rackhir let her lead the way across the strange terrain and Lamsar followed him.

Sorana and Rackhir had been lovers once, in Yeshpotoom-Kahlai, the Unholy Fortress where evil blossomed and was beautiful. Sorana, sorceress, adventuress, was without conscience but had had high regard for the Red Archer since he had come to Yeshpotoom-Kahlai one evening, covered in his own blood, survivor of a bizarre battle between the Knights of Tumbru and Loheb Bakra's brigand-engineers. Seven years ago, that had been, and he had heard her scream when the Blue Assassins had crept into the Unholy Fortress, pledged to murder evil-makers. Even then he had been in the process of hurriedly leaving Yeshpotoom-Kahlai and had considered it unwise to investigate what was obviously a death-scream. Now she was here—and if she was here, then it was for a strong reason and for her own convenience. On the other hand, it was in her interests to serve Chaos and he must be suspicious of her.

Ahead of them now they saw many great tents of shimmering grey which, in the light, seemed composed of all colours. People moved slowly among the tents and there was an air of leisure about the place.

'Here,' Sorana said, smiling at him and taking his hand, 'the Grey Lords hold impermanent court. They wander about their land and have few artifacts and only temporary houses which you see. They will make you welcome if you interest them.'

'But will they help us?'

'You must ask them.'

'You are pledged to Eequor of Chaos,' Rackhir observed, 'and must aid her against us, is that not so?'

'Here,' she smiled, 'is a truce. I can only inform Chaos of what I learn of your plans and, if the Grey Lords aid you, must tell them how, if I can find out.'

'You are frank, Sorana.'

'Here there are subtler hypocrisies—and the subtlest lie of all

113

is the full truth,' she said, as they entered the area of tall tents and made their way towards a certain one.

In a different dimension of the Earth, the huge horde careered across the grasslands of the North, screaming and singing behind the black-armoured horseman, their leader. Nearer and nearer they came to lonely Tanelorn, their motley weapons shining through the evening mists. Like a boiling tidal wave of insensate flesh, the mob drove on, hysterical with the hate for Tanelorn which Narjhan had placed in their thin hearts. Thieves, murderers, jackals, scavengers—a scrawny horde, but huge...

And in Tanelorn the warriors were grim-faced as their outriders and scouts flowed into the city with messages and estimates of the beggar army's strength.

Brut, in the silver armour of his rank, knew that two full days had passed since Rackhir had left for the Sighing Desert. Three more days and the city would be engulfed by Narjhan's mighty rabble—and they knew there was no chance of halting their advance. They might have left Tanelorn to its fate, but they would not. Even weak Uroch would not. For Tanelorn the Mysterious had given them all a secret power which each believed to be his only, a strength which filled them where before they had been hollow men. Selfishly, they stayed—for to leave Tanelorn to her fate would be to become hollow again, and that they all dreaded.

Brut was the leader and he prepared the defence of Tanelorn—a defence which might just have held against the beggar army—but not against it and Chaos. Brut shuddered when he thought that if Chaos had directed its full force against Tanelorn, they would be sobbing in Hell at that moment. A sliver of luck there was in the Unbreakable Law which governed both Law and Chaos and forbade them direct attack on men. They *had* to use human agents for their work.

Dust rose high above Tanelorn, sent flying by the hooves of the scouts' and messengers' horses. One came through the gate as Brut watched. He pulled his mount to a stop before the nobleman. He was the messenger from Kaarlak, by the Weeping Waste, one of the nearest major cities to Tanelorn.

The messenger gasped: 'I asked Kaarlak for aid but, as we

supposed, they had never heard of Tanelorn and suspected that I was an emissary from the beggar army sent to lead their few forces into a trap. I pleaded with the Senators, but they would do nothing.'

'Was not Elric there—he knows Tanelorn?'

'No, he was not there. There are rumours that he was killed in a great sea-battle between the Trader-princes of the Purple Ports and the Lormyrian Confederation, that the fleets met off Sorcerer's Isle near the Yellow Coasts and that the Trader-princes smashed the strength of Lormyr, slaying Elric in the process. There is another rumour which said that he was badly wounded and now lies dying among the ruins of Imrryr, his own city which he, himself, destroyed. But all I know is that Zarozinia, his princess, mourns him for dead and we'll get no help from Elric or from Kaarlak in Elric's name.'

Brut was pale.

'What of Jadmar—will Jadmar send warriors?' The messenger spoke urgently, for many had been sent to the nearer cities to solicit aid.

'I do not know,' replied Brut, 'and it does not matter now—for the beggar army is not three days march from Tanelorn and it would take two weeks for a Jadmarian force to reach us. We are doomed.'

'And Rackhir?'

'I have heard nothing and he has not returned. I have the feeling he will not return—Tanelorn is doomed.'

Rackhir and Lamsar bowed before the three small men who sat in the tent, but one of them said impatiently: 'Do not humble yourselves before us, friends—we who are humbler than any.' So they straightened their backs and waited to be further addressed.

The Grey Lords assumed humility, but this, it seemed, was their greatest ostentation, for it was a pride that they had. Rackhir realised that he would need to use subtle flattery and was not sure that he could, for he was a warrior, not a courtier or a diplomat. Lamsar, too, realised the situation and he said:

'In our pride, Lords, we have come to learn the simpler truths which are only truths—the truths which you can teach us.'

The speaker gave us a self-deprecating smile and replied:

'Truth is not for us to define, guest, we can but offer our incomplete thoughts. They might interest you or help you to find your own truths.'

'Indeed, that is so,' Rackhir said, not wholly sure with what he was agreeing, but judging it best to agree. 'And we wondered if you had any suggestions on a matter which concerns us—the protection of our city, Tanelorn.'

'We would not be so prideful as to interfere our own comments. We are not mighty intellects,' the speaker replied blandly, 'and we have no confidence in our own decisions, for who knows that they may be wrong and based on wrongly assessed information?'

'Indeed,' said Lamsar, judging that he must flatter them with their own assumed humility, 'and it is lucky for us, Lords, that we do not confuse pride with learning—for it is the quiet man who observes and says little who sees the most. Therefore, though we realise that you are not confident that your suggestions or help would be useful, none the less we, taking example from your own demeanour, humbly ask if you know of any way in which we might rescue Tanelorn?'

Rackhir had hardly been able to follow the complexities of Lamsar's seemingly unsophisticated argument, but he saw that the Grey Lords were pleased. Out of the corner of his eye he observed Sorana. She was smiling to herself and it seemed evident, by the characteristics of that smile, that they had behaved in the right way. Now Sorana was listening intently and Rackhir cursed to himself that the Lords of Chaos would know of everything and might, even if they did gain the Grey Lords' aid, still be able to anticipate and stop any action they took to save Tanelorn.

The speaker conferred in a liquid speech with his fellows and said finally: 'Rarely do we have the privilege to entertain such brave and intelligent men. How may our insignificant minds be put to your advantage?'

Rackhir realised quite suddenly, and almost laughed, that the Grey Lords were not very clever after all. Their flattery had got them the help they required. He said:

'Narjhan of Chaos heads a huge army of human scum—a beggar army—and is sworn to tear down Tanelorn and kill her inhabitants. We need magical aid of some kind to combat one so powerful as Narjhan *and* defeat the beggars.'

'There are beetles in Kaleef,' said a Grey Lord who had not spoken before, 'which emit a peculiar venom.'

'Beetles, Lord?' said Rackhir.

'They are the size of mammoths,' said the third Lord, 'but can change their size—and change the size of their prey if it is too large for their gullets.'

'As for that matter,' the first speaker said, 'there is a chimera which dwells in mountains South of here—it can change its shape and contains hate for Chaos since Chaos bred it and abandoned it with no real shape of its own.'

'Then there are four brothers of Himerscahl who are endowed with sorcerous power,' said the second Lord, but the first interrupted him:

'Their magic is no good outside our own dimension,' he said. 'I had thought, however, of reviving the Blue Wizard.'

'Too dangerous and, anyway, beyond our powers,' said his companion.

They continued to debate for a while, and Rackhir and Lamsar said nothing, but waited.

Eventually the first speaker said:

'The Boatmen of Xerlerenes, we have decided, will probably be best equipped to aid you in defence of Tanelorn. You must go to the mountains of Xerlerenes and find their lake.'

'A lake,' said Lamsar, 'in a range of mountains, I see.'

'No,' the Lord said, 'their lake lies above the mountains. We will find someone to take you there. Perhaps they will aid you.'

'You can guarantee nothing else?'

'Nothing—it is not our business to interfere. It is up to them to decide whether they will aid you or not.'

'I see,' said Rackhir, 'thank you.'

How much time had passed since he had left Tanelorn? How much time before Narjhan's beggar army reached the city? Or had it already done so?

Suddenly he thought of something, looked for Sorana, but she had left the tent.

'Where lies Xerlerenes?' Lamsar was asking.

'Not in our world,' one of the Grey Lords replied, 'come we will find you a guide.'

117

Sorana spoke the necessary word which took her immediately into the blue half-world with which she was so familiar. There were no other colours in it, but many, many shades of blue. Here she waited until Eequor noticed her presence. In the timelessness, she could not tell how long she had waited.

The beggar horde came to an undisciplined and slow halt at a sign from its leader. A voice rang hollowly from the helm that was always closed.

'Tomorrow, we march against Tanelorn—the time we have anticipated is almost upon us. Make camp now. Tomorrow shall Tanelorn be punished and the stones of her little houses will be dust on the wind.'

The million beggars cackled their glee and wetted their scrawny lips. Not one of them asked why they had marched so far, and this was because of Narjhan's power.

In Tanelorn, Brut and Zas the One-handed discussed the nature of death in quiet, over-controlled tones. Both were filled with sadness, less for themselves than for Tanelorn, soon to perish. Outside, a pitiful army tried to place a cordon around the town but failed to fill the gaps between men, there were so few of them. Lights in the houses burned as if for the last time, and candles guttered moodily.

Sorana, sweating as she always did after such an episode, returned to the plane occupied by the Grey Lords and discovered that Rackhir, Lamsar, and their guide were preparing to leave. Eequor had told her what to do—it was for her to contact Narjhan. The rest the Lords of Chaos would accomplish. She blew her ex-lover a kiss as he rode from the camp into the night. He grinned at her defiantly, but when his face was turned from her he frowned and they went in silence into the Valley of the Currents where they entered the world where lay the Mountains of Xerlerenes. Almost as soon as they arrived, danger presented itself.

Their guide, a wanderer called Timeras, pointed into the night sky which was spiked by the outlines of crags.

'This is a world where the air elementals are dominant,' he said. 'Look!'

Flowing downwards in an ominous sweep they saw a flight

118

of owls, great eyes gleaming. Only as they came nearer did the men realise that these owls were huge, almost as large as a man. In the saddle Rackhir strung his bow. Timeras said:

'How could they have learned of our presence so soon?'

'Sorana,' Rackhir said, busy with the bow, 'she must have warned the Lords of Chaos and they have sent these dreadful birds.' As the first one homed in, great claws grasping, great beak gaping, he shot it in its feathery throat and it shrieked and swept upwards. Many arrows fled from his humming bow-string to find a mark while Timeras drew his sword and slashed at them, ducking as they whistled downwards.

Lamsar watched the battle but took no part, seemed thought-ful at a time when action was desired of him.

He mused: 'If the spirits of air are dominant in this world, then they will resent a stronger force of other elementals,' and he racked his brain to remember a spell.

Rackhir had but two arrows left in his quiver by the time they had driven the owls off. The birds had not been used, evidently, to a prey which fought back and had put up a poor fight con-sidering their superiority.

'We can expect more danger,' said Rackhir somewhat shakily, 'for the Lords of Chaos will use other means to try and stop us. How far to Xerlerenes?'

'Not far,' said Timeras, 'but it's a hard road.'

They rode on, and Lamsar rode behind them, lost in his own thoughts.

Now they urged their horses up a steep mountain path and a chasm lay below them, dropping, dropping, dropping. Rackhir, who had no love for heights, kept as close to the mountainside as was possible. If he had had gods to whom he could pray, he would have prayed for their help then.

The huge fish came flying—or swimming—at them as they rounded a bend. They were semi-luminous, big as sharks but with enlarged fins with which they planed through the air like rays. They were quite evidently fish. Timeras drew his sword, but Rackhir had only two arrows left and it would have been useless against the air-fish to have shot them, for there were many of the fish.

But Lamsar laughed and spoke in a high-pitched, staccato

119

speech. *'Crackhor—pishtasta salaflar!'*

Huge balls of flame materialised against the black sky—flaring balls of multicoloured fire which shaped themselves into strange, warlike forms and streamed towards the unnatural fish.

The flame-shapes seared into the big fish and they shrieked, struck at the fire-balls, burned, and fell flaming down the deep gorge.

'Fire elementals!' Rackhir exclaimed.

'The spirits of the air fear such beings,' Lamsar said calmly.

The flame-beings accompanied them the rest of the way to Xerlerenes and were with them when dawn came, having frightened away many other dangers which the Lords of Chaos had evidently sent against them.

They saw the boats of Xerlerenes in the dawn, at anchor on a calm sky, fluffy clouds playing around their slender keels, their huge sails furled.

'The boatmen live aboard their vessels,' Timeras said, 'for it is only their ships which deny the laws of nature, not they.'

Timeras cupped his hands about his mouth and called through the still mountain air: 'Boatmen of Xerlerenes, free-men of the air, guests come with a request for aid!'

A black and bearded face appeared over the side of one of the red-gold vessels. The man shielded his eyes against the rising sun and stared down at them. Then he disappeared again.

At length a ladder of slim thongs came snaking down to where they sat their horses on the tops of the mountains. Timeras grasped it, tested it and began to climb. Rackhir reached out and steadied the ladder for him. It seemed too thin to support a man but when he had it in his hands he knew that it was the strongest he had ever known.

Lamsar grumbled as Rackhir signalled for him to climb, but he did so and quite nimbly. Rackhir was the last, following his companions, climbing up through the sky high above the crags, towards the ship that sailed on the air.

The fleet comprised some twenty or thirty ships and Rackhir felt that with these to aid him, there was a good chance to rescue Tanelorn—if Tanelorn survived. Narjhan would, anyway, be aware of the nature of the aid he sought.

Starved dogs barked the morning in and the beggar horde, waking from where they had sprawled on the ground, saw Narjhan already mounted, but talking to a newcomer, a girl in black robes that moved as if in a wind—but there was no wind. There was a jewel at her long throat.

When he had finished conversing with the newcomer, Narjhan ordered a horse be brought for her and she rode slightly behind him when the beggar army moved on—the last stage of their hateful journey to Tanelorn.

When they saw lovely Tanelorn and how it was so poorly guarded, the beggars laughed, but Narjhan and his new companion looked up into the sky.

'There may be time,' said the hollow voice, and gave the order to attack.

Howling, the beggars broke into a run towards Tanelorn. The attack had started.

Brut rose in his saddle and there were tears flowing down his face and glistening in his beard. His huge war-axe was in one gauntleted hand and the other held a spiked mace across the saddle before him.

Zas the One-handed gripped the long and heavy broadsword with its pommel of a rampant golden lion pointed downwards. This blade had won him a crown in Andlermaigne, but he doubted whether it would successfully defend his peace in Tanelorn. Beside him stood Uroch of Nieva, pale-faced but angry as he watched the ragged horde's implacable approach.

Then, yelling, the beggars met with the warriors of Tanelorn and, although greatly outnumbered, the warriors fought desperately for they were defending more than life or love—they were defending that which had told them of a reason for living.

Narjhan sat his horse aside from the battle, Sorana next to him, for Narjhan could take no active part in the battle, could only watch and, if necessary, use magic to aid his human pawns or defend his person.

The warriors of Tanelorn, incredibly, held back the roaring beggar horde, their weapons drenched with blood, rising and falling in that sea of moving flesh, flashing in the light of the red dawn.

Sweat now mingled with the salt tears in Brut's bristling beard and with agility he leapt clear of his black horse as the screaming beast was cut from under him. The noble war-cry of his forefathers sang on his breath and, although in his shame he had no business to use it, he let it roar from him as he slashed about him with biting war-axe and rending mace. But he fought hopelessly for Rackhir had not come and Tanelorn was soon to die. His one fierce consolation was that he would die with the city, his blood mingling with its ashes.

Zas, also, acquitted himself very well before he died of a smashed skull. His old body twitched as trampling feet stumbled over it as the beggars made for Uroch of Nieva. The gold-pommelled sword was still gripped in his single hand and his soul was fleeing for Limbo as Uroch, too, was slain fighting.

Then the Ships of Xerlerenes suddenly materialised in the sky and Brut, looking upward for an instant, knew that Rackhir had come at last—though it might be too late.

Narjhan, also, saw the Ships and was prepared for them.

They skimmed through the sky, the fire elementals which Lamsar had summoned, flying with them. The spirits of air and flame had been called to rescue weakening Tanelorn. . .

The Boatmen prepared their weapons and made themselves ready for war. Their black faces had a concentrated look and they grinned in their bushy beards. War-harness clothed them and they bristled with weapons—long, barbed tridents, nets of steel mesh, curved swords, long harpoons. Rackhir stood in the prow of the leading ship, his quiver packed with slim arrows loaned him by the Boatmen. Below him he saw Tanelorn and was relieved that the city still stood.

He could see the milling warriors below, but it was hard to tell, from the air, which were friends and which were foes. Lamsar called to the frisking fire elementals, instructing them. Timeras grinned and held his sword ready as the ships rocked on the wind and dropped lower.

Now Rackhir observed Narjhan with Sorana beside him.

'The bitch has warned him—he is ready for us,' Rackhir said, wetting his lips and drawing an arrow from his quiver.

Down the Ships of Xerlerenes dropped, coursing downwards on the currents of air, their golden sails billowing, the warrior crews straining over the side and keen for battle.

Then Narjhan summoned the *Kyrenee*.

Huge as a storm-cloud, black as its native Hell, the *Kyrenee* grew from the surrounding air and moved its shapeless bulk forward towards the Ships of Xerlerenes, sending out flowing tendrils of poison towards them. Boatmen groaned as the coils curled around their naked bodies and crushed them.

Lamsar called urgently to his fire elementals and they rose again from where they had been devouring beggars, came together in one great blossoming of flame which moved to do battle with the *Kyrenee*.

The two masses met and there was an explosion which blinded the Red Archer with multi-coloured light and sent the Ships rocking and shaking so that several capsized and sent their crews hurtling downwards to death.

Blotches of flame flew everywhere and patches of poison blackness from the body of the *Kyrenee* were flung about, slaying those they touched before disappearing.

There was a terrible stink in the air—a smell of burning, a smell of outraged elements which had never been meant to meet.

The *Kyrenee* died, lashing about a wailing, while the flame elementals, dying or returning to their own sphere, faded and vanished. The remaining bulk of the great *Kyrenee* billowed slowly down to the earth where it fell upon the scrabbling beggars and killed them, leaving nothing but a wet patch on the ground for yards around, a patch glistening with the bones of beggars.

Now Rackhir cried: 'Quickly—finish the fight before Narjhan summons more horrors!'

And the boats sailed downwards while the Boatmen cast their steel nets, pulling large catches of beggars aboard their Ships and finishing the wriggling starvlings with their tridents or spears.

Rackhir shot arrow after arrow and had the satisfaction of seeing each one take a beggar just where he had aimed it. The remaining warriors of Tanelorn, led by Brut who was covered in sticky blood but grinning in his victory, charged towards the unnerved beggars.

Narjhan stood his ground, while the beggars, fleeing,

streamed past him and the girl. Sorana seemed frightened, looked up and her eyes met Rackhir's. The Red Archer aimed an arrow at her, thought better of it and shot instead at Narjhan. The arrow went into the black armour but had no effect upon the Lord of Chaos.

Then the Boatmen of Xerlerenes flung down their largest net from the vessel in which Rackhir sailed and they caught Lord Narjhan in its coils and caught Sorana, too.

Shouting their exhilaration, they pulled the struggling bodies aboard and Rackhir ran forward to inspect their catch. Sorana had received a scratch across her face from the net's wire, but the body of Narjhan lay still and dreadful in the mesh.

Rackhir grabbed an axe from a Boatman and knocked back the helm, his foot upon the chest.

'Yield, Narjhan of Chaos!' he cried in mindless merriment. He was near hysterical with victory, for this was the first time a mortal had ever bested a Lord of Chaos.

But the armour was empty, if it had ever been occupied by flesh, and Narjhan was gone.

Calm settled aboard the Ships of Xerlerenes and over the city of Tanelorn. The remnants of the warriors had gathered in the city's square and were cheering their victory.

Friagho, the Captain of Xerlerenes, came up to Rackhir and shrugged. 'We did not get the catch we came for—but these will do. Thanks for the fishing, friend.'

Rackhir smiled and gripped Friagho's black shoulder. 'Thanks for the aid—you have done us all a great service.'

Friagho shrugged again and turned back to his nets, his trident poised. Suddenly Rackhir shouted: 'No, Friagho—let that one be. Let me have the contents of that net.'

Sorana, the contents to which he'd referred, looked anxious as if she had rather been transfixed on the prongs of Friagho's trident. Friagho said: 'Very well, Red Archer—there are plenty more people on the land,' pulled at the net to release her.

She stood up shakily, looking at Rackhir apprehensively.

Rackhir smiled quite softly and said: 'Come here, Sorana.' She went to him and stood staring up at his bony hawk's face, her eyes wide. With a laugh he picked her up and flung her over his shoulder.

'Tanelorn is safe!' he shouted. 'Come, Sorana—you shall learn to love its peace with me!' And he began to clamber down the trailing ladders that the Boatmen had dropped over the side.

Mayflower Occult Books for your enjoyment

MAGIC: AN OCCULT PRIMER	David Conway	75p ☐
ASTROLOGY AND SCIENCE	Michael Gauquelin	40p ☐
THE SYBIL LEEK BOOK OF FORTUNE TELLING	Sybil Leek	35p ☐
THE NATURAL HISTORY OF THE VAMPIRE	Anthony Masters	50p ☐
ETERNAL MAN	Pauwels & Bergier	50p ☐
THE MORNING OF THE MAGICIANS	Pauwels & Bergier	50p ☐
WHAT YOUR HANDS REVEAL	Jo Sheridan	35p ☐
THE GREAT BEAST	John Symonds	60p ☐
A HANDBOOK ON WITCHES	Gillian Tindall	35p ☐
THE MINDBENDERS	Cyril Vosper	40p ☐
THE OCCULT	Colin Wilson	£1.00 ☐

All these books are available at your local bookshop or newsagent; or can be ordered direct from the publisher. Just tick the titles you want and fill in the form below.

━━

Name..

Address ....

....

Write to Mayflower Cash Sales, P.O. Box 11, Falmouth, Cornwall TR10 9EN. Please enclose remittance to the value of the cover price plus 10p postage and packing for one book, 5p for each additional copy. *Granada Publishing reserve the right to show new retail prices on covers, which may differ from those previously advertised in the text or elsewhere.*